THE WEREWOLF ON LOWRE FEW LANE

Bryce Bentley-Tales

A NineStar Press Publication

Published by NineStar Press
P.O. Box 91792,
Albuquerque, New Mexico, 87199 USA.
www.ninestarpress.com

The Werewolf on Lowre Few Lane

Printed in the USA
First Edition
October, 2018

Print ISBN: 978-1-949340-29-7

Also available in eBook, ISBN: 978-1-949340-07-5

Warning: This book contains sexually explicit content, which may only be suitable for mature readers.

Thirteen-year-old Colton and his best friend Jade spend their free time investigating a local urban legend concerning an old abandoned house in their hometown in Ireland. The run-down building is said to be haunted and some of the things they've seen seem to confirm it.

Colton has a crush on foreign-exchange student, Dylan, who is visiting his aunt from America. But Dylan isn't your average American kid, and soon Colton and his friends are embroiled in more than urban legend and must find a way to save everything they know and love.

To my avid reader–Mom. A book you can read without the nightmares.

Chapter One

I ROTATED THE zoom dial on my binoculars. The three-story stone house loomed large in my view.

Jade whispered behind me, "Colton, what'd you see?"

"Shhh."

I surveyed the gloomy home from side to side. The house sat on the crest of a small hill and far from the cobbled street where I crouched. Spidery cracks filled a couple of the second-story windows. The paint had faded and peeled, and the rooftop sections were missing shingles. It had to be one of the oldest residences in Arklow.

"Colton," Jade said, tapping my shoulder.

"Jade, you're breaking me concentration."

Huddled near the stone column at the end of the winding driveway, I inched around the base a bit farther to get a better look. A light, cool breeze blew, swaying the sea of tall weeds in the house's lawn and filling my nose with the scent of dogs.

Deep, guttural barks erupted behind me. Startled, I whirled before realizing that the noise was just Jade's ringtone. I glared while she squatted close to the curb, frantically patting the outside of her lightweight jacket in search of her phone.

"Are you a complete tool? Turn the blimey thing off."

Jade glanced up, her eyes wide. "Can't find it." Then she straightened, grinned at me, and said, "Found it." She removed the phone from a side pocket, and the barking grew in volume. Brushing her lengthy brown hair from her face, she stared at the caller ID. "Oh...it's me mum."

"Shut it off! All of Ireland will know we're here!"

She didn't move but held the smartphone in both palms. The phone quit ringing finally, and she sighed. "I should go. It's probably suppertime."

"You can't. This was your idea."

A loud clanging echoed across the yard, and we both cowered behind the stone fence post. Adjacent to the old post, a crumbling stone wall shielded us from anyone standing by the house. When I poked my head around the ledge, nothing but the motionless tall weeds could be seen in the yard and the same gloomy look the house had had before. It was dead quiet.

Jade put her hands on my shoulders, her mouth next to my ear. "S-see, I told you. You believe me now? It's haunted."

I tried to speak, but my mouth was dry. I brought my binoculars up, gripping them hard with both hands.

"Probably just varmint inside," I said.

"Aye. And maybe you and your butterfingers could be captain of the rugby team."

"Har-har. You think the Kennedy twins really disappeared inside?"

"I told you. I saw them at the house when I was with Erin two nights ago. They said they were going inside."

"Maybe they're hanging out at the local pub downtown?"

"Colton, no one has seen those fellas since that night. They went inside and never came out, sure of it."

I swiveled the binoculars around, peering at the large, arched front doorway, which had a wolf face doorknocker.

Jade whispered close to my ear, "You see anything?"

"Shhh, I can't focus with your tongue in my ear."

"My tongue isn't in your ear," Jade said, her voice irritated.

After a few seconds, she pushed on my shoulder. "By the way, you find out the new foreign-exchange fella's story? You didn't take your eyes off him in class. I missed a lot while I was away." She giggled. "You fancy him, don't you?"

I cringed, lowered the binoculars, and spoke in a hushed voice over my shoulder. "Don't say that out loud."

"And who's going to blimey hear us? Just us and the ghouls at 44 Lowre Few Lane."

"Dylan. That's his name. We've spoken barely a couple of words since he started. I took him to Headmaster Collin's office on his first day and managed to say hello. And for your knowledge, he *is* right bloody in front of the board. I can't help but look in his direction."

"Mm-hmm," Jade said.

I started to bring my binoculars back up when Jade said, "Well, I like his accent. Oh, I think he noticed you after school today. Did you see that? Maybe he likes boys too. You never know." She swatted my back. "Are you blushing?"

I shook my head. My face was hot, though. I had seen Dylan outside talking to a couple of boys on the rugby team. Our eyes had met, but I'd been quick to look away.

I shifted my weight on my knees. Jade now leaned against my back, and it was getting hard to bear her weight.

"Oh, Colton, you are so darling sometimes. I missed you while I was gone the last two weeks."

"It's been bloody miserable," I said. "I've eaten lunch a couple times with Thomas until he was sent to detention. Tried to eat with Erin, but she just smiles at me."

"Well," Jade said, "I'm back now. So we'll eat lunch together. Where's Dylan from again?"

I opened my mouth to say he was from America but never got a chance. A barking ringtone erupted again. I jumped a foot in the air and whipped my head toward Jade. She brought out her phone and stared at it.

I put my hands on my hips and snarled, "Oh for bloody sake, Jade. You can't be serious. Put it on vibrate."

Jade held her finger up, stepped to the curb, and answered her phone. "Mum?"

I sighed, leaning my back against the stone column.

"No," Jade said. "I'm fine. Just out of breath. I'm with Colton." Jade stared at me, the end of her mouth curled down. "Oh, Mum. You've too met him. You had him over for dinner five times this summer. He's the Asian?" Jade rolled her eyes. "Mum, that's who I just said. *Colton*. It is too what I said. And it's not impolite. He is half-Asian. Remember, you thought it right peculiar his mother was from Singapore and the father Irish, asking me how they ever met." She looked at me before turning away and lowering her voice. "Uh, no, Mum. He can't hear me."

She walked away from me, but her voice still carried. "No, Mum, we haven't seen any packs of dogs. No." She turned back, giving me an inquisitive look.

I shook my head. Over the last week, I had heard from a couple of friends there had been sightings of a pack of dogs, but that was just rumor.

"Colton hasn't seen any either."

I looked at the horizon and down the cobbled road. The few homes in this part of Arklow stood far off the roadway and scattered about, giving off a sense of remoteness. With the sun turning reddish and less than an hour from setting, that isolation magnified the creepy vibe from the small wood surrounding the manor we'd come to investigate. We needed to go.

I whirled my finger in the air for Jade to hurry it up. She stood in the middle of the road, held up a hand to me, and offered a nervous smile. She told her mother, "We stayed after school and helped Ms. Griffin with decorations in the auditorium. *Yes*, for Hollow's Eve. It's tomorrow, remember?" Jade fussed with her hair while she talked. "Oh, Mum, good grief, you met her too. She's me sixth-grade history teacher. Sings in the town choir?"

Rubbing the back of my neck, I sighed and took a quick gander back at the house from my vantage point. I raised the binoculars and peered at the porch. A couple of rickety boards stuck up. Close to the bottom steps, on either side, gray wolf statues sat back on their hindquarters. They stared straight ahead in my direction.

A shadow crossed over one of the statues. I moved the binoculars a hair to the right. A black-haired wolf crouched at the statue's base, its amber eyes pointed in my direction. I stepped back and tripped over my feet, landing on a cushion of waist-high grass.

Jade knelt down to my side. "Colton, what is it?" She no longer had the phone to her ear.

I pointed to the house. "W-w-wolf."

Jade's eyes widened. "Wolf?" She stared toward the house, shaking her head. "I don't see anything. You mean the statues?"

I got up to my feet and tugged on her hand. "L-let's go."

"Okay, good," Jade said. "I told Mum we're going home."

As I glanced over my shoulder, the black wolf was gone, but I remained fixated on the statues. I took in a sharp breath. The statues were no longer staring straight ahead, but instead, the snout of one of the wolf statues was up in the air as if howling. The second one's head was turned toward me.

I sprinted with everything I had.

Chapter Two

SEVERAL MOMENTS LATER, I stopped at the peak of the hill and bent over to catch my breath. A few old stone-and-brick homes were nestled off the road.

Jade was still several feet behind and came up at a trot. I looked down the cobbled street at the home below. The house was shrouded in shadows, and an army of sinister slender dark trees reached over the roof to block my view.

Jade called after me, out of breath. "Colton, wait up."

She leaned her forearm against a tree near a curb. Her cheeks flushed red and her green eyes flared. "You saw a wolf?"

I ran my hand through my hair. I decided I must have been seeing things. Statues can't move. I told her about the live wolf I had seen. "It was black, and its eyes glowed."

Jade stepped toward me, smoothing the creases in her pants. "Hmmm. And it wasn't some grungy dog? Never heard of wolves in these parts."

A boy's voice spoke from behind me. "Thought I heard someone."

Jade and I hollered in unison. I spun around. A boy my height stood in front of me, wearing a red ball cap, his dark curly hair pushing out from the hat's bill.

"Dylan," I managed in a hoarse voice.

Dylan grinned and dimples formed in his cheeks. He came forward. "Wha's up? What're you doing? Don't you both live, like, far from here?" He was still wearing his school khaki pants but had changed into a T-shirt that said *No Haters Allowed.*

"W-we," I stammered. My mind was blank.

Jade jabbed her finger downhill and spilled the truth. "We came to spy on that house down there. It's haunted, you see."

"Haunted?" Dylan said.

"Aye," Jade said. "Me friend and I had been this way a couple nights ago to go over to her cousin's home. We heard strange noises come from inside. Howling and screaming. And a couple of lads, the Kennedy twins, came up and decided to go inside. They haven't been seen since."

"Oh." Dylan glanced down the slope toward the house. "That's scary."

"Bloody right, it's scary," I said.

"You saw them go inside?" Dylan asked.

"Well," Jade said and rubbed her chin with one hand. "We saw them reach the porch."

"What are you doing here?" I asked Dylan and looked around. It seemed peculiar that Dylan would be here. Most students lived anywhere but in this area. This was an old part of town that had mostly older residents.

Dylan fixed his hat on his head, one side of his mouth turned downward in a frown, and he looked up in contemplation. "What was I doing?" He jabbed his index finger up in the air, and his gaze met mine. "Oh, I remember. I was fixing up my room. My aunt wants it spic and span. She's a drill sergeant on some things but chill about other stuff. It's crazy." He shook his head and laughed. "She really isn't that bad, though. Whatever you do, don't tell her I said she was strict. Okay?"

Jade and I exchanged looks, and then we both nodded at the same time. I asked, "You live close by?"

Dylan took his hat off, and curls toppled in his face. He brushed them out of his eyes. "I live over there." He pointed to a small brick house that was about twenty feet downhill. "It's much smaller than my home in the US."

Jade slapped my arm. "You never told me he was a Yank!"

I gritted my teeth, and my face felt hot. I was going to until her phone had interrupted me.

Dylan chuckled. "A Yank. I've never been called that. That's funny. I'm from Portland."

"Portland is a county back in America?" Jade asked.

"No," Dylan said and laughed. "It's a city. You ever heard of Oregon?"

I glanced to Jade, and she shrugged. I turned back to Dylan, feeling inadequate, all of a sudden wishing I knew more about America. I shook my head.

Dylan said, "It's right below Washington."

"Oh, I've heard of Washington," I said, a smile spreading across my face. "That's where your president lives." It felt good to be able to impress Dylan.

Dylan shook his head and opened his mouth like he was going to protest. But he was interrupted by a woman's voice.

"*Dylan!*"

Dylan looked over his shoulder and back to us. He put his hat back on. "That's my aunt. Hey, you want to come inside?"

"We can't—" Jade started.

I pinched her arm, and she jumped. I hissed through my teeth, "Just for a wee moment."

Jade fixed her hair and offered her best pleasant smile. "Oh, that'd be smashing, Dylan. I will need to call me mum to say we'll be a little later. And Colton, you need to call your dad."

Dylan led us back down the cobbled street. The three-story manor at the far bottom was still out of sight. The lean trees spread around it gave me glimpses of a couple of dark windows that glared at me, and I was convinced that that was what death's eyes looked like.

Dylan's house was not far. He turned into a yard and stepped over a narrow rock walkway up to the porch.

Jade asked, "Sooo, it's just you and your aunt?"

Dylan's hand was on the doorknob, and he turned toward us. "Well, my parents are in Portland. They sent me here to be close to my roots. I guess their parents emigrated from here when they were just children."

I looked up to the top of the door and startled. On it was an iron wolf doorknocker similar to the one on the haunted house we had been spying on. The wolf's jaw was opened in a snarl, and long fangs extended out. Next to the doorframe was a worn sign that sat askance on the wall and had the number *50*. I surmised Dylan's address was 50 Lowre Few Lane.

Dylan let us inside and called out, "Aunt Ruth, I'm home."

The savory scent of cooked lamb filled my senses. A woman's voice called from where the wonderful smell emanated.

"Where you run off to, you rascal? You need to tell me when you go messing about." Aunt Ruth came out from the kitchen area. Her white hair was made up in a bun, large glasses sat on her nose, pronounced creases in her forehead. Her eyes widened, seeing Jade and me, and she scolded Dylan. "Oh lad, you didn't tell me you had guests coming over for supper. No matter, it's good to see you making friends at school. We have more than enough for everyone to eat."

Jade held up her hand. "Oh, beg your pardon, ma'am, but we don't want to be a bother. We—"

"Ohhh, it's no bother, lass. I'm Ruth Burns. What are your names?"

"I'm Jade."

"Colton," I said and gave her a small wave.

"You both will stay for supper, won't you?"

Jade shrugged. "I just need to make sure it's okay with me mum."

"Me too," I said. "But it won't be a problem. Mum is out on work for the next two weeks, and me dad has been busy with his job."

"Oh," Aunt Ruth said. "What do your parents do?"

"Mother is a chemical engineer and travels for her job. Dad is a supervisor for that new airline company. UK Air Stars."

"Oh, that sounds like some fine work. Well, we'd be happy to have you. And of course, I'll give you a ride home afterward. Besides, you children should not be walking about right now."

Jade pushed my arm. "Told you."

Aunt Ruth turned to Dylan, placing her hands on her hips. "Mister, take that hat off in this house. And I've seen your room, young sir. Let these two wash up and call their folks, and you best get that room in order."

Dylan looked over at us, shrugged, and smiled, then headed to his room.

After Jade and I had gotten permission to stay for dinner from our parents, we washed our hands and followed Aunt Ruth to the dining room.

I moseyed behind Jade and Aunt Ruth and admired black-and-white photographs on the wall while Aunt Ruth asked Jade questions. "Tell me about your family, lass. What do they do?"

Jade made quote gestures with her fingers. "Me mum calls it 'administrative clerk,' but she works at the local shampoo manufacturer. They distribute worldwide. Me father and mother divorced a couple of years ago. He lives in York now, but I visit him in the summer. I just came from his place this week in fact."

"Oh, went to visit?"

"No, I was at a wake for my grandmother. I got back three days ago. I was really tired, and me mum didn't make me go to school until today. I just formally met Dylan for the first time a few minutes ago."

I had stopped in the hallway and stared at a framed photograph. It was of a teenage boy and girl who stood by a horse carriage, and right behind them was a porch. They looked similar and were probably brother and sister.

"Colton?" Dylan's voice called from behind me. I jumped and turned to him.

Dylan smiled. "Oh, sorry. That's the second time I made you jump. Come on. Try my aunt's cooking. You'll be way impressed."

I followed him and glanced one more time at the photograph. I recognized the gray wolf statues by the porch. They sat back on their hindquarters, staring straight ahead.

The supposed brother and sister were standing in front of the house on 44 Lowre Few Lane.

Chapter Three

AUNT RUTH SERVED us mouth-watering lamb on our plates. She sat down at the opposite end of the table from Dylan and waved her hand for everyone to start. I forked a juicy piece of meat into my mouth, and it took restraint to keep myself from eating at an impolite greedy pace. My grandmother had cooked us some memorable dinners, but this one took the cake. Not to mention my dad had been late from work the last couple of nights, and I had been cooking my own meals.

Dylan sat at the end of the table, glanced up in my direction a couple of times, and smiled.

Jade said between mouthfuls, "Ms. Ruth, this is wonderful."

Dylan asked Jade, "You're in my history class, too, right? Ms. Griffin's?"

Jade wiped her mouth with her napkin. "One row over and three seats back."

"Oh," Dylan said and gave a short laugh. "That's like real specific. My bad. I just started early October, but you've been gone, right?"

Jade nodded. "Yes. I had to go over to England for a wake."

"Oh," Dylan said, speaking through a mouthful. "Sorry."

I asked Dylan, "You just arrive from America this month?"

Dylan forked in a new heap and answered cheerfully, "Oh heck no. I've been here since June."

He glanced over to his aunt. She quit eating, crossing her arms over her chest, and her eyes became narrow slits. He slowed his chewing and looked down at his plate.

"But, it's almost Hollow's Eve," Jade observed.

Dylan barely chewed his food, his cheeks puffed out, and he continued to stare down. He turned to Jade. "I know. Messed up, huh?"

I caught Jade's eyes, asking, "But what have you been doing the whole time?"

Dylan replied, "Oh, well, that's a real good question." His face flushed red.

Aunt Ruth spoke. Her voice had a harsh bite. "Dylan, it's impolite to speak with your mouth full. Why don't you get everyone some bread? I forgot it by the stove."

"What? Oh, yeah, cool." Dylan was up in a second and went into the kitchen area.

Aunt Ruth asked, "You both like some more potatoes?"

I put my hand up. Aunt Ruth passed a bowl over, and I dipped several browned potatoes out onto my plate.

Aunt Ruth informed Jade and me, "I was going to be visiting me brother in Brighton when Dylan arrived this summer. Me brother was very ill. I had Dylan attend the boarding school at Wexford Secondary while I was away. I just returned late September. So..." Aunt Ruth shrugged. The ends of her mouth curved upward, and her face softened. "I had Dylan come back here with me and start school here. It's grand having him."

Dylan came out of the kitchen carrying a plate with a loaf of bread on top and set it down on the table. Aunt Ruth told Dylan, "I was telling them about the boarding school down in Wexford. The one you've been attending while I was in England."

"Oh, right." Dylan sat back down and spoke with sarcasm. *"The boarding school."*

"What was the school called again?" I asked Dylan.

Dylan looked up at me and glanced back to his aunt. Aunt Ruth said, "Wexford Secondary."

Dylan slapped his forehead. "Swear, man, my head would fall off if it wasn't attached."

"Did you like the boarding school?" Jade asked.

Dylan nodded. "Oh, I guess it rocked."

I said, "I had a cousin that graduated from there last year. He played rugby too. I see you play after lunch. You're really good. Did you play at the other school?"

Dylan ate his bread and said with a neutral tone, "Oh, yeah, cool sport. Hated to leave my team there." That nonchalant comment did not seem genuine. *Is he lying?*

I turned to Aunt Ruth. "How is your brother?"

Aunt Ruth had taken a piece of bread from the plate and looked over to me, her brow furrowed in confusion.

"You said he was ill."

Aunt Ruth chuckled. "Oh, now he is doing fine. Very kind of you to ask."

Dylan blurted out. "Jade and Colton think two boys disappeared in the house down the road."

"Oh." Aunt Ruth sat back in her chair. One of her hands lay on the table, and her fingers tapped one after the other. "And you say these boys went inside 44 Lowre Few Lane?"

Jade leaned forward and blabbed. "Me friend Erin and I walked by the house two nights ago. We were cutting through to see Erin's cousin, to introduce me. When we went by the house, we heard noises inside."

"What did you hear?" Aunt Ruth asked. Her tone no longer had any hint of amusement.

Jade looked over to me as if I had the answer. I shrugged. She turned back to Aunt Ruth. "They were banging noises inside. Like someone was blimey remaking the interior. Then there was howling. We started to run away when we saw the Kennedy lads come up, and we warned them to leave. They're a lot older, though, and told us to scoot off."

"I've heard of the Kennedy brothers," Aunt Ruth said. "In their twenties. They're not chisellers like yourself. And why were these brothers there?"

Jade's eyes were large and her voice animated. "They said they were going inside to investigate."

Aunt Ruth leaned forward on the table, and asked Jade, "How were they going to investigate? They tell you?"

"They had some equipment they had taken from a local TV studio that's used for ghost houses. Said they were going to test the paranormal energy waves. Brian, that's one of the brothers. He said the place was haunted by a spirit named Ronan. Someone who had lived there long ago."

"And no one has seen the brothers since," I said, remembering that Jade had told me that.

Aunt Ruth brought her hands into her lap, her eyes distant and her mouth pursed together. "No doubt the lads have meandered off to a new adventure. Probably over in that town of Limerick that has received international news for its haunted homes." She flapped her hands at Jade and I and said, "Well, I think it's late, and your family will be wanting to know where you're at. I'll take you home." She turned to Dylan. "Why don't you help with the dishes?"

Dylan rolled his eyes, scooted his chair back, and pumped his fist up in the air. "Yes. Dishes." He turned to me and lifted his fist up to me. "Well, dude, see you later."

I stared down at his knuckles and back to him, uncertain what I was supposed to do.

He laughed and said, "Don't be such a playa. Make a fist and stick it up." I did, and he bumped his knuckles against mine and laughed. It was contagious, and I chuckled too. He bumped fists with Jade, and she giggled.

I asked him, "Are you going to the Hollow's Eve dance tomorrow night?"

"You should come!" Jade said and hopped up and down. "The girls will just love it!" She looked at me and shrugged. "Well, they will."

His eyes opened wide, and he turned to his aunt. "Forgot all about that. Can I?"

Aunt Ruth sighed. "Don't see why not." She wagged her finger at him. "But I'll drive you there and pick you up."

He turned to Jade. "Cool. Tomorrow, I'll be sure to say hi in history class." He disappeared into the kitchen.

Aunt Ruth told Jade and me to go outside and get into the car. I started out to the car but went to the bathroom first. I washed my hands, and on my way to the front door, I paused at the doorway of a study and observed Aunt Ruth by a tall hutch. She reached up to the top and brought something down in a closed fist. She opened her hand and a few gold coins lay in her palm.

She turned her head to me. I flinched, and she nodded, saying in a stern voice, "I'll be right out."

I blushed and hurried outside. I sat down in the back of the sedan and put on my seat belt.

Jade looked over the seats up to the front of the house. She spoke in a hushed voice. "It seem a bit peculiar in there? Like there's something brooding under the surface?"

I shrugged. "I guess." I slapped my forehead. "Forgot me blimey book bag." I was out of the car and halted outside the front door. Loud voices carried from inside.

Aunt Ruth was talking. "You're not to ever go near that house again."

Dylan whined, "I didn't!"

"No lies, Dylan!"

"Lies! Ha! You should talk!"

"Go to your room, sir. Your parents sent you here to keep you out of mischief, not make more of it. I'll be back in a few, and I expect you in that bed and asleep." Her voice drew closer to the front door.

I wheeled around, ran back to the car, opened the back door, and sat down hard. I fumbled with my seat belt and clicked it on. I felt Jade's eyes burning into me, and I turned to her.

She threw her hands up in the air. "Where's your blimey bag, you dote?"

I faced forward. "It's okay. I don't really need it. It just has some school books."

"What do you mean you don't really need it?" Jade asked.

Aunt Ruth came out the front door, and she held my book bag in one hand.

"Colton," Jade said, shaking her head. "Sometimes you can act the regular neddy."

Chapter Four

THE MORNING OF the next day, my alarm blurted out an annoying bray. I hit the snooze, rolled over, and fell fast asleep again. Ten minutes later, the clamorous ringing was back. My hand fumbled on the nightstand, and the noise shut off.

My father's voice spoke through the door. "Colton."

I pulled my sheet over my head.

My door cracked open. "Are you awake? Son, you hear me?"

"Yes," I croaked, pulling the sheet tight over my head.

"Get up. You need to catch the bus this morning. I can't take you. Too much to do at work."

"Okay." I sat up on the edge of my bed, my sheet still draped over my head.

"I have to travel up to Dublin today. I might need to stay the night."

I nodded.

"Do you hear me, Colton?"

"*Yes.*"

"Well, get your bum in gear. I'll hire Georgia to stay the night if I do stay over. Be sure to take your cell phone with you, and I'll call you one way or the other."

I groaned. "Nooo. Not her. She's completely off her rocker."

"Look, Colton. Your mum will be back in over a week, and she won't be traveling for a while, and my job will get better. It's just really busy right now. We'll take some family time together and maybe travel through Europe."

I moaned and nodded. My door clicked closed, and I fell back on the bed. A second later, the door reopened. "Oh, Colt. Mister, take that blanket off your head."

I pulled my sheet off my head and sat up. My father's head poked around the door. His blond hair was combed neatly back, and he had his usual day's growth of beard on his face.

"Happy Hollow's Eve."

My eyes widened. Today was Hollow's Eve. "Dad, I can still go to the Hollow's Eve dance, right?"

Dad frowned and scratched his chin. "I suppose so. Georgia will take and pick you up, though. Colton, look up here. I don't want you walking around after school anymore. Those Kennedy twins have gone missing, and there are reports of some kind of wild dog packs around."

I nodded. "Okay, Dad." Then blurted out without thinking, "Can I have a friend stay over too?"

Dad raised one gray brow. "Who? Thomas? Better if your mum or I'm here. That boy sometimes acts without thinking."

"No, not him. Dylan."

"Oh. Is that who you ate dinner with last night?"

I nodded and smiled. "He's from America."

"America? That's a pond away, isn't it?" Dad's phone rang in his pocket, and he took it out, stared at the caller ID, and nodded to me. "Okay, Colton. I suppose he can if his folks say it's okay. But just do everything Georgia tells you. And you need to get to school. I got too much on me mind right now and don't need the extra stress of taking a call from Headmaster Collins."

Dad pulled my door closed as he answered his phone.

I bolted out of bed and hopped up and down. I pumped my fist in the air and hollered, "Yes!" I did a quick jig I had been practicing every night when I listened to my favorite pop band.

I was going to see Dylan at the party tonight, and then he would stay the night. The first thing I would do when I got to school would be to ask him to sleep over. That way he'd have plenty of time to ask permission from his aunt.

I headed toward the bathroom but froze in the hall. The memory of Aunt Ruth scolding Dylan was in my mind. Dylan's aunt seemed to think Dylan was getting into mischief. Would Aunt Ruth say yes? She was allowing him to come to the dance tonight, so how strict could she really be?

I went into the bathroom and stared at my reflection in the mirror. My hair stood up in every direction. I splashed water over my face, wet my hair, and then combed it forward. I leaned up and stared at my nose. I was the only boy at our school to have darker skin but still managed to have freckles on the end of my tiny nose.

I grinned. A new idea came to me. Maybe if Aunt Ruth said no, she would compromise and let me stay the night at Dylan's house. Then I could avoid seeing the babysitter, Georgia, and get to be with Dylan. It was a win-win situation.

Twenty minutes later, I ran out of my front door. My father's sedan was already gone. With a slice of bread with jelly in one hand, I made it to the corner just as the bus turned at the end of the street and headed in my direction. Butterflies swirled in my stomach on the ride to school, and I played in my head how I would ask Dylan to stay overnight.

What was the word Dylan used? *Dude.* And don't forget *man* and *playa.*

"Morning, dude. Hey, man, you want to stay the night over at my house after the party? It'd be sweet to have you, playa. We could try out my badminton set and play my new card game. Saturday, we'll meet Jade to play some croquet over at Erin's house and act the regular maggots. It'll be so much fun."

I slapped my head. Leave out maggots. That was not an American thing to say.

When the bus arrived, I hurried off, jogged into the school, and stood on my tiptoes, looking over everyone's heads. A gangly youth with uncombed bright red hair was walking toward me. Thomas. He didn't just tower over me but was taller than most of my classmates. About to turn fourteen, he was a year older than me, and I had heard he had been held back three years ago. His blue-collared school shirt was unbuttoned at the top, and his freckled face and huge nose were as eye-catching as his personality.

He grinned at me and pumped his fists in the air. "Colton, I won most valued player on the hockey team." He honked out laughter and slapped my arm.

"Oh, that's great, Thomas." I scanned the area, searching for Dylan.

Thomas continued to speak, but the words made little impression. "And you hear about the temperature drop?"

I grunted, "No."

I spotted Dylan's dark curly hair. My stomach did a somersault. He was talking to three of the rugby players. He held up his fist to the boys, gesturing for them to hit it with their knuckles. The boys looked at him and at each other. Dylan taught them his strange American custom of bumping fists. The rugby boys swatted Dylan's arm and laughed.

"Colton?"

I looked over to Thomas. His eyes narrowed, his bottom lip pulled up over the top. "Where's your mind swimming up there?" His finger tapped my forehead.

"What? Oh, I just have stuff to do. What were you saying?"

Thomas sighed. "I said we're goin' to need our coats pretty soon. It's going to be freezing."

I patted his chest and returned my gaze to Dylan, who made goodbye hand-bumps to the rugby players.

"Great, Thomas. I have to go. But let's talk at lunch. And congratulations on the, uh, hockey thing."

My feet carried me to Dylan.

Thomas spoke at my back. "But I got detention again."

I glanced over my shoulder, put my hand up in the air, and waved. My shoulder thudded into someone. I snapped around in time to see I had bumped into one of the boys who had been talking to Dylan. The boy dropped his books.

John. That was his name. A boy with a slender nose with thick brown hair. Once upon a time, I had blushed any time this cutie came around, until I caught an air of his contempt.

He was staring at me with slit eyes and his hands on his hips. "Watch where you're walking, chink-chink. It's a good thing I need you for maths, otherwise..." He punched his fist into his hand.

I muttered, "O-oh sorry." I bent down and picked up his books, and he snatched them away. John and the other boys wheeled around and stepped away.

My shoulders slumped, and I came up to Dylan's back. He was crouched down at his locker, rummaging through his books. Several girls laughed hard next to me. They were looking over at Dylan and whispering conspiratorially to each other.

"Dylan." My voice was barely audible to my own ears with the girls' giggling off the side drowning it out. But even so, Dylan's head bobbed up as if he had heard something, and he glanced over his shoulder. A grin spread over his face, and he stood up, holding his books.

"Hey, dude. Wha's up?"

"What?" I furrowed my brow and looked up at the ceiling, confused.

Headmaster Collins walked down the hall, the light gleaming off his shiny bald head, and said, "Get to your class. You've got fifteen more minutes. No excused tardies."

Dylan glanced to the headmaster and then back to me. A small smirk was on his face. "It means how are you?"

"Oh, I'm fine."

"What class you going to?"

"German."

"They have German here? Cool. Which way?"

I pointed. My tongue had forgotten how to work.

"That's sweet," Dylan said. "I'm going the same way."

I walked by his side, and we passed the gaggle of girls. He waved to them. "Wha's up, ladies?" A few put hands over their mouths, and a roar of high-pitched giggles erupted at our backs.

"Is it me," Dylan said and glanced over his shoulder for a second, "or are the girls a little off here?"

"Off?" I shook my head. "Those girls?"

"Yeah, they're a bit weird."

"Don't mind them tools," I said. "The school should offer a semester seminar on how to understand the pre-teen lass."

Dylan laughed and stopped close to a door. "No doubt." He looked toward the doorway where a couple of students entered, then back to me. "So, I'll see you tonight at the

Hollow's Eve party? A couple of girls asked if I was going. But these chicks give me a headache. It'd be cool to hang out with you and—what was her name?—Jade. Or are you going with someone?"

"Yes!" I said, excited, and then shook my head. "I mean no. I'm just going with Jade. But we're not actually together."

Jade came up beside me and clapped Dylan on his shoulder. "Hey, player." She giggled with her hand over her mouth. She looked at us both with a grin. "Heard my name."

I never got to say anything. We all froze at Ms. Griffin's voice calling Jade's name and mine. "Mr. Ryan and Ms. O'Reilly."

I turned around. Ms. Griffin was wearing a bright purple blouse that day, and as usual, her hair was pulled back into a long ponytail.

"Mr. Foley said he saw you both walking around yesterday on Lowre Few Lane?" she asked.

Jade nodded. "Y-yes, ma'am."

I pointed my finger to Dylan. "We went to his house."

She looked to Dylan and narrowed her eyes. "Mr. Payne. You live out there?"

Dylan gave an easy smile. "Yes, ma'am."

She scratched her chin. "Well, I'll be. All you children need to be careful right now. I heard they had loose dog packs. Never heard of wild dogs being in Ireland."

"Five minutes," the headmaster called from down the hall.

Ms. Griffin waved to us and said, "See you in history class."

Jade touched my arm and Dylan's and leaned forward. "Lads, I got something to tell you."

The headmaster came over and said, "Ms. O'Reilly. May I have a moment of your time? I understand you are considering the master choir." He looked to Dylan and me, saying, "Get to class, lads. Or detention for the both of you."

She whispered to me, "Well, I'll tell you when you get to class." She walked in step with the headmaster down the hall.

Dylan watched her walk away and turned to me. "She's cool. Well, I better get to class. Hey, saw you scored high in math. Killin' it, dude." He grinned. "Wait, you don't know that saying either, do you?"

I slowly shook my head.

He held his fist up. "Don't be such a playa. Hey, maybe we can sit together at lunch?"

I bumped his fist, and he turned around and started toward his class before I could answer. "Dylan!"

He stopped and looked back at me, his dark eyebrows raised. A couple of girls stood behind him, including Erin. She wiggled her fingers at me.

I ignored Erin, stepped closer to Dylan, and whispered, "Uh, c-can you stay the night? I mean, over at my house. If you're not busy, that is. I'm just wondering..."

A grin spread over Dylan's face, the dimples in his cheeks pronounced. "That'd be sweet. Let's see what the Battle Axe says, though. I'll work my magic." He waved at me. "Later." He stepped through the door.

I walked on air to my class. Dylan had not only said he would sit by me at lunch, but he might also spend the night. We'd see each other at the dance, and then... A fog of doubt crept into my mind. I was uncertain whether I should be excited or disappointed. Would the stayover actually happen? An image of a Battle Axe was in my mind. I had no idea what Dylan's last comment meant, unless he meant his aunt was the Battle Axe?

I entered my classroom and beelined it to my chair.

Jade came up to my side. "Okay, so did you hear?"

"Hear what?"

"The Kennedy twins?"

I sat down and shook my head. "No, what?"

"They found one of the brothers walking in the neighborhood we were at yesterday. He was cold as ice too."

"How'd you find this out?"

"Erin's mum is a nurse and just called her to warn her to take the bus straight after school. Erin says they took him to the nearby hospital, and he's in a deep sleep. But he kept repeating one word over and over."

"What?" I asked.

"Werewolf."

Chapter Five

LUNCHTIME CAME, AND I headed to the cafeteria. I scanned the room, searching for Dylan. My heart beat fast. I didn't see him. Nor did I see anyone I wanted to sit with, or someone, for that matter, who would want me to sit next to them.

Ms. Griffin was standing close to several teachers, and I picked up bits and pieces of the gossip. You could count on Ms. Griffin for gathering the latest scandal regarding students, teachers, and anything else, and sometimes she would let things slip to students. Especially if she liked them. She was talking about Brian and the fact that he and his brother had been at *that house*. I assumed she meant 44 Lowre Few Lane.

Boys' laughter reached my ears and I turned. On the far side of the room sat a row of the rugby players. My heart plummeted to depths of glumness. Dylan was sitting with them, his back to me. Several of the boys were laughing at whatever story Dylan was telling them.

I got my lunch, my head hung down, and I clomped down the hall to go outside. A few boys were forming up teams for rugby and asking for players.

A round-faced boy pointed toward me and asked, "What about him?"

I froze in place. A skinny, spindly-legged boy cawed in laughter and slapped the oval-faced lad on the back. "Don't be a muppet. He's only good at running numbers in his head."

The two boys faced away from me and continued their search for players.

Always singled out as the smart kid. The brainy one. Tears threatened to spill, but I kept control and headed to my favorite oak tree. I had no chance of winning over Dylan. The thought of Dylan made my heart flitter. Dylan would usually come outside to play.

"Colton, wait," Jade called from behind me.

I turned and Jade caught up to me, carrying her lunch tray in her hand.

Erin was a step behind her, a bag lunch in one hand, and said, "Heya, Colton." She brushed her blonde-red locks from her eyes, cocked her head to the side, a thin smile forming over her face. Her eyelashes flittered up and down at a rapid rate.

"Uh, do you have something in your eyes?" I asked.

She grinned as if I had told her she was the most beautiful creature I've ever seen. Her two large front teeth were glaring. The space between them was at least a good Irish mile. I gave her a half smile, and a nervous laugh spilled out.

"I heard you're going to the dance tonight, Colton," she said.

"Oh," I answered. "Aye, I am. You?"

Her eyelashes somehow fluttered even faster, and I was certain the wind speed would knock me off my feet. She pulled her bottom lip over her top, making a pouty face. "I hope you save the song 'Give Me Your Hand' just for me. We danced to it last year. Remember, Colton?" A gleek of spittle spurted out between her two front teeth and hit my cheek. I rubbed it off with the back of my hand in a subtle manner, not wanting to hurt her feelings.

"Oh, right," I squeaked. "That'd be brilliant."

I turned away and looked down at the ground for a good spot to sit and get out from Erin's gaze. Erin not only seemed to be immune to the *Dylan-craze*, but she also had no inkling I had zero interests in girls. Jade was the only one who knew I liked boys. My friend Thomas had told me he had a gay uncle, and I think he suspected I was too. But we had never talked about it. Maybe a couple of teachers had their suspicions too?

I sat down on the ground and leaned against the large oak. Jade took a seat by my side. Erin stared at the grassy ground, appearing uncertain where to plant her bottom.

"Oh," I said. "Here." I took my jacket off and put it down for her. I regretted it a second later. She grinned from ear to ear and sat down, fixated on me.

I looked away and found an interesting bush close to the school to stare at. I ate some roasted beef on bread. Jade told Erin about our interesting venture the night before.

"Oh my." Erin touched her chest. "I passed the house last night, too, to see my cousin. Gives me the creeps, it does. I feel like those stone wolf statues are watching me. Just frightening to think those boys disappeared inside."

I turned to Jade. "That Kennedy brother say anything else?"

"That's all I heard. You think when he says werewolf, he's talking of the same wolf you saw last night?"

I shrugged. "Don't know. He's okay, though?"

Jade put up both hands.

"Mum says he's out now. Can't rouse him up," Erin said between bites. She glanced between Jade and me and spoke with a mouthful of pudding. "And you saw a real wolf, Colton?" Liquid squirted between her teeth and dribbled over her bottom lip, which she wiped away a second later. She reached out and touched my knee. "You must have been so scared."

"Um..." I stared down at her hand lying placidly on my knee. "I think it was just a grungy dog."

A shadow moved over me and a voice spoke with a shrill edge. "Well, look at you scallywags."

I looked up to discover my good friend, Thomas. He wiped his huge nose and waved down at me.

"I thought you were in detention?" I asked.

Thomas plopped down in front of me. "'Course I was." Thomas laughed. "But some lass was barreling down the hall, effin' and blindin' about some dogs on campus. Mr. Foley ran out the door and told her to quit her hollering. But she just kept her blathering. He didn't come back, and I decided I'd had enough detention for the day."

The noise of boisterous boys yelling reached us. Several of the rugby players ran outside to a small field near us. One boy was throwing a ball to another. Dylan came out of the school with three others, and everyone was animated. He walked in our direction, then glanced at me, caught my eyes, and I choked. He brought his hand up and smiled, then turned away and formed up on teams with the boys and started playing.

"Colton, you neddy," Thomas said in front of me.

I turned to him. My face felt hot. "What?"

"Is your mind up in them clouds again? You hear they turned that scrapper into the rugby captain?"

I shook my head. "Who?"

Thomas cawed with laughter. "Who you think, you plonker. That Yank. Connor's out with a bad arm, so they needed a new captain."

Jade was surprised. "He's been here barely the month of October!"

I stared over at the game. Dylan sprinted down the field. He hugged the ball to his side, faked right, and skirted with ease around two boys who fell to the ground on top of each other. He leaped over a tackling peer, landed on the other side at a dead run, and flipped the ball easily to a squat boy next to him.

A couple of boys tried to tackle some stout player but ended up hanging on each leg. The stocky player tossed the ball back to Dylan, but it was a bad throw. Dylan slowed to a jog, put up his hand, and stopped the ball in midair with his palm. At the same time, a broad-shouldered boy came in for the easy takedown. Everything looked like it was not just over for Dylan, but it was going to be a fumble. But Dylan scooped the ball into his side in one smooth motion, wheeled on his tiptoe, and did a complete three-hundred-sixty-degree turn. The heavyset boy flew past, unable to stop. Dylan flipped the ball to another mate on his side who made it another few feet before someone locked their arms around his waist and took him down.

"That," Thomas said, his tone genuinely awed, "was bleedin' deadly!"

I nodded, my mouth dry, and turned to Jade. Her eyes were glazed over. She stared at Dylan with ferocious eyes I felt must be akin to a fox watching a chicken in a henhouse.

Erin offered me a much too sweet smile. "He told me they can't play like that in America."

I furrowed my brow. "Play like what?"

"Play rough like."

"Yes, they do," I said, my tone rising. "They just call it football." Why was Dylan talking to Erin?

She smiled, appearing content to know something I didn't. She shook her head. "Aye. But only with helmets and gear on. After lunchtime, they play something called tag football. He told me this when he walked me to my cousin's. Lives close by, he does. Then he sat down with me at lunch too. He done it three times now. I looked for you, Colton, but you were nowhere in sight." She smirked and said, "You should come to the lunchroom more often. Don't know what you might miss."

Spittle flew from her mouth and smacked into my nose. I wiped it away, and this time, I was not subtle.

"And when he walked with me to my cousin's, he said he would go with me to Dublin in December. Invited me to America, he did. Said I could fish out in the ocean by his city. What's it called? Oregon?" she continued.

"Portland," I hissed. "He lives in the state of Oregon. Right below the state of Washington where the president lives."

Erin tipped her head back and guffawed. Thomas jumped and turned around to look at Erin.

"What the bloody—" Thomas started to say.

"What are you laughing about?" I asked, interrupting Thomas. I gritted my teeth and leaned forward.

Jade was looking between Erin and me, her expression alarmed. Erin put her hand over her mouth, her back bucking with laughter. She giggled between her fingers. In between breaths, she said, "Washington, DC, is where the president lives, and it's on the East Coast of America. Don't you know anything?"

"So?" I said and glanced to Jade. She gave me an empathetic look.

Erin shook her head with her hand still over her mouth and then dropped it to her lap. Her two large front teeth fully in view. The canyon between them was far too conspicuous.

She grinned wide. "You're such a plonker."

"Oh," Thomas said, raising his eyebrows. "Lass just put you on the spot."

I turned to Jade. "You have any bloody idea what she's blathering on about?"

Jade nodded. "Washington, DC, is on the East Coast. But the state of Washington is on the West, and Oregon is right below it."

I growled, "*What?* You knew that and didn't tell me yesterday? Dylan probably thinks I'm a complete tool."

Thomas jerked his head back and laughed, then looked over, drew his eyebrows inward, and asked me, "You didn't know there are two Washingtons? Even I know that, and, chap, you're Asian."

Erin chirped in, a full grin on her face. "Aye, poor Colton didn't know. Not sure if Dylan thinks you're a tool, but he said he liked smart lasses. And he said he'd show me Seattle, too, which, so you know, is in the state of Washington. I think Dylan fancies me. Can't blame him, can you?" She leered over at me.

I balled my hands into fists and unclenched them a second later. I sat up straighter and said, "Well, be sure if you all kiss, you don't drink any water so your mouth is dry as leather. Otherwise, you might drown the poor fella with the canyon up in your mouth."

Erin's eyes widened and her hands flew up over her mouth. "Y-you're a..." she stammered. She got up to her feet, tears falling down her cheek. "You're a maggot!"

Jade got up on her knees. "Erin, wait—"

Erin cried harder and sprinted off past the oak, across the field where the rugby game was playing. I smirked as she fled. The rugby ball rolled in front of her, and a boy leaped in the air and fell down on top of it. A couple of boys piled on him. Erin threw her hands up in the air and shrieked out loud. She fell back onto her butt. Her crying was audible from where I sat, and my smirk faltered.

The boys who had fallen on the ball were up on their knees, staring at Erin with large befuddled eyes. Several rugby boys came over, and many of them crossed their arms as Erin cried hysterically. A few of them chuckled nervously.

Erin had her hands over her mouth and screamed at them. "You're all maggots!"

Several of the boys laughed. Erin's cries grew in crescendo and she fled, disappearing around a row of trees. I swallowed the bile in my throat. The triumphant feeling I'd had was now hollowed.

I looked over at Jade. She had her hands on her hips, and her eyes were slits. "Colton Ryan! You should be ashamed of yourself."

Jade stormed past the tree, and my eyes watered.

Thomas leaned over and socked my arm in a friendly gesture. "I thought you were bloody brilliant."

I nodded, tried to smile.

"Everyone! Inside!" a voice boomed out.

Headmaster Collins stood at the front door, and several teachers swerved around him, gathering students near the door.

Ms. Griffin's eye-catching purple top was in view. She grabbed a couple of boys and shoved them toward the door and then beelined it toward the field, yelling, "Stop the game! Everyone inside!"

"What is this holy show?" Thomas muttered.

I shook my head. "I don't know. They never rang the bell."

Ms. Griffin was waving to the rugby players who had not quit playing and yelled in a commanding voice, "Stop that game at once!"

The boys all froze and stared at her. A shaved-headed boy whined, "But the bell hasn't rung, ma'am."

Ms. Griffin opened her mouth, but what she was about to say, I have no idea. A harsh shriek echoed out from across the field, on the other side of a row of trees. My heart beat fast. That was the direction Erin had gone...and Jade.

I was up on my feet and running across the field toward the line of trees. I barely heard Thomas or Ms. Griffin calling out my name.

I almost slowed when Dylan called out. Another scream came again, this time more shrill. Was that Jade? Or Erin? I wasn't certain, but I ran harder.

Chapter Six

I RACED ACROSS the field and yelled, "*Jade!*"

I came to the end of the row of trees.

Jade's unsteady voice on the other side commanded, "D-don't move, Erin."

I darted around the edge of the trees. Erin and Jade were not far away, huddled close together and with arms interlocked around each other. Their backs were to me.

Over their shoulders, I made out four snow-white wolves crouched low to the ground and spread out twenty feet in front of them. Snarls distorted each of their snouts. Their black eyes focused on the two girls.

I came to a sudden halt, but my momentum carried me so that I stumbled forward. My hands flew out to keep my balance, and my fingertips touched close to Jade's foot.

Jade and Erin jumped, and Erin gave a short, high-pitched shriek. The wolves jolted at my unexpected arrival too. Their growls grew in crescendo, and they fixed their stares on me.

I reached out, grabbed Jade's arm and Erin's, and pulled. "Run!"

One wolf sprang forward, and the others followed.

The girls did not need any prodding. They bolted forward. I came around the tree edge, but the school looked so far away. I glanced over my shoulder. Erin and Jade were on my heels, their eyes wide in terror. The white wolves careened around the edge of the trees, traveling at an unbelievable pace.

I turned forward. My mind was in overdrive, my heart racing, and I had tunnel vision. I forgot Jade or Erin and stared helplessly at the school building in the distance. A few students had not gone inside and were watching us. I recognized Thomas's red hair. A couple of teachers who had stayed outside were gawking at us too. I recognized Ms. Griffin's short purple coat as she ran toward me.

I glanced over to my right. A figure low to the ground barreled fast from the school. I tried to discern what I was seeing, but it was a blur. A black wolf.

I fell backward. Erin and Jade tripped over me and fell to the ground. I put my hands up defensively to the charging wolf, but the animal vaulted up and soared high over my head. I whipped around to see it land on the opposite side of me and come up in a defensive position. The white wolves came to an abrupt stop, and all of them crouched low to the ground. None moved, but the steady growls were audible.

I pushed Jade and Erin off me, got up, and crawled backward toward the school building, keeping my attention on the wolves. The girls glanced to me and then back to the soon-to-be wolf brawl, and then they were up on their hands and knees, following me. After a few feet, I stood, and Jade came up next. I helped Erin to her feet and towed her toward the school. Jade was next to me, and we hurried toward Ms. Griffin who was now making a full-out dash to us, holding the hem of her dress up. A tumultuous roar of yelps and barks erupted behind me, and I looked over my shoulder to see that the white wolves had attacked the black one.

Ms. Griffin reached us, out of breath, and she cried, "Get in the school now!"

I ran forward. Erin and Jade were at my side. Ms. Griffin was at our backs, prodding us forward. The rest of the students, having seen the pack of wolves, had fled into the school.

The headmaster stood at the open door, waving to us. *"Get inside! Come on!"*

I glanced over my shoulder one more time. The four white wolves lay on the ground and then got back up to their wobbly feet and scurried away in the opposite direction. The victorious black wolf stood with its legs apart, its head stooped and back hairs raised.

I ran inside the door, followed by Jade, Erin, and Ms. Griffin. The door slammed shut behind us.

Headmaster Collins told Ms. Griffin, "Get them to the gym. Each teacher needs to take roll of their home class."

Mr. Foley came toward us, his eyes wide. "Headmaster Collins. The teachers have taken roll. Besides these students here, we're missing one from my class. Dylan Payne."

I stopped, and Jade ran into my back.

Ms. Griffin tugged on my arm. "Come on, child."

"No," I said, shaking my head. "We have to go get him."

Headmaster Collins narrowed his eyes and pointed down the hall. "Mr. Ryan, you get to that gym now."

I put my head down, and Ms. Griffin pulled me forward. We rounded a corner, and ruckus youth noises drifted from the gym ahead. Erin was now sobbing at my side, wiping her eyes. Jade's face was pale white, her eyes vacant, and she was wiping her hands on her shirt over and over.

The door at the end of the hall was half-opened. Thomas poked his head through, then stepped out and came up to us. "Are you all completely mental? You were almost dinner."

Ms. Griffin addressed Thomas. "Mr. O'Leary, where's your homeroom? That is where you should be right now."

Thomas shrugged. "Can't say, Ms. Griffin. Everyone is acting like a bunch of yobos in there."

Ms. Griffin sighed and ushered us into the gym, then closed the door behind us. "This day just wears on," She muttered, then stepped in front of us and hollered for several boys to quit running up and down the bleachers.

I crossed my arms, a lump in my throat and my stomach somersaulting. My entire body trembled. Tears streamed down Erin's cheeks. Jade put her arm around her shoulders, trying to comfort her. Thomas was the only one with no hint of a terror-stricken persona. He'd also not almost been eaten by wolves.

Thomas leaned in. "You're lucky, mate, that other wolf showed up and didn't think you looked like a scrumptious rabbit."

Students milled in the gym. Several chased one another in a game, teachers attempting to get order. I overheard several of the rugby boys ask where Dylan went.

John shoved a boy's shoulder, saying, "He was right in front of you!"

I looked up to Thomas. He massaged the back of his neck, watching the pandemonium in front of us, too, and uttered, "You think they'd now give me some time off with the detentions. These rascals in here need one worse than me."

"Did you see him?" I asked.

Thomas turned to me. "Who?"

I slapped Thomas's arm. "Dylan, you clonk!"

Thomas grinned. "Oh, right. Well, at least I know where Washington DC is."

I socked him harder. *"Thomas! Did you see him or not?"*

He furrowed his brow and rubbed his arm. "Ouch." His eyes lit up and pointed behind me. "Right there."

I wheeled around. Dylan had opened the door from the hall and walked into the gym. He was buttoning his shirt, which was in complete disarray.

"Dylan!"

I hurried to him. His shirt was untucked and wrinkled, his shoes untied. He looked up at me, his bangs in front of his eyes. He pushed his hair out of the way and picked a few black hairs from his now-wrinkled white shirt, then offered me a half grin.

"Hey, man."

"Where were you?"

He pointed his thumb over his shoulder. "Oh. The bathroom." He looked over my shoulder. "Oh, did something happen? What'd I miss, dude?"

"*What'd you miss?*" I asked, flabbergasted.

Jade called from behind me. "Dylan!" She came up to my side, her arms crossed over her chest and her eyes narrowed. "Where have you been? Everyone is looking for you!"

"Oh." Dylan's smile faded. "I-I—"

"Mr. Payne," Ms. Griffin said as she came up to my other side. "Where did you go? And why are your shoes on the wrong feet?"

Dylan snapped his gaze down, then looked back up, his face red. He stepped out of his shoes, putting them on the correct way, and gave a nervous chuckle. "I thought they felt weird."

Thomas made a goofy laugh and told Ms. Griffin, "Chap was in the loo."

Dylan looked at Thomas, confused. "Loo? I said I was in the bathroom."

Thomas laughed. "That's what I just blimey said."

Several of the rugby player boys cried out behind us and hurried over.

"Dylan!"

"Where were you?"

"Where'd you go?"

Ms. Griffin shook her head and held her hands up to the rugby boys. "Young men, he can answer your questions later. Mr. Payne, you need to come with me. Headmaster Collins is organizing a search party at this moment."

"Oh." Dylan scratched his head. "He is?"

She tugged on his hand, taking him toward the door, which flew open at that second. Headmaster Collins and Mr. Foley stood in the doorway, their eyes huge saucers. Headmaster Collins saw Dylan and sighed. Then he wiggled his index finger, beckoning Dylan. Dylan stepped forward, glancing over his shoulder to me before turning back and disappearing with Headmaster Collins into the hallway.

Jade leaned over and whispered, "Colton. Was that the same black wolf you saw at the house last night?"

I nodded, my gaze meeting hers. "I think it was."

I looked back down where Dylan had taken his shoes off. There were more black hairs that had tumbled to the floor.

Chapter Seven

IT HAD BEEN an hour, and most of the students in the gym had departed. The school had been closed early, and parents had been requested to pick up their children. After the bizarre sighting of the stray pack of wolves, the school was not running any of the buses but required every student to be signed out by an adult. The dance for the night had been postponed to a later date, and rumors surfaced it might be altogether cancelled.

Ms. Griffin was talking closely to a teacher and fussing that Ireland had never seen the likes of this before. Her high-pitched voice carried. "Wolves? Strangest sight. Maybe from some zoo?"

I sat on one end of the gym with Thomas and Jade. Jade sat with her back against the wall and played a game on her phone. Thomas twirled his hair, headphones in his ears, mouthing a song. Erin's mother had already come, so she was gone.

My babysitter, Georgia, was on her way. Jade was unable to reach her mother. Jade remembered that her mother was taking new investors on a tour of the plant and had told her to call her cousin Janine if she needed anything. Except Cousin Janine was not answering.

Dylan had not returned to the gym, or his aunt might have already gotten him. I didn't know.

Disappointment did not quite describe how I felt. I was demoralized. I had not only looked forward to seeing Dylan that night at the dance, but then we were going to have the sleepover at my house. My plans for card games, badminton, croquet, and acting the maggots had been dashed.

I was playing with a deck of cards by myself. I set them in my book bag and asked Jade, "You think those white wolves came from inside that house? Like the black wolf?"

Jade stopped playing on her phone and looked up at me with confusion. "What? Why would you ask that?"

"Well, no one has ever seen white wolves in these parts or, for that matter, anywhere in Ireland or all of the United Kingdom. Where else would they come from?"

"I just heard Ms. Griffin say they could have come from a zoo?" Jade observed.

I leaned over and said in a quiet tone, "But they could have come from that house too?"

Jade cocked her head to the side. "But how do white wolves come from a house on Lowre Few Lane, Colton?"

I shrugged.

Thomas took his earphones out of his ears and asked in an animated voice, "Did you say you saw them wolves at Lowre Few Lane?"

"No," Jade said. "We never saw wolves. Well, I mean, Colton said he saw that black wolf."

Thomas pointed his finger up in the air. "Forty-four Lowre Few Lane? That place?"

"How did you know?" I asked.

"Oh," Thomas said, squawking out his goofy laugh. "It's a well-known haunted house. And I've seen those statues by the porch. Creeps is what they give me." He leaned over. "Me uncle once told me that somewhere inside the house is a magical doorway to another world."

Ms. Griffin's voice spoke from above us. "Did I hear that you kids were at 44 Lowre Few Lane?"

I glanced to Jade, who had wide eyes, and then looked up to Ms. Griffin. My shoulders caved in. "Aye. We did."

Jade spoke at a fast pace. "It's the last place where I saw the Kennedy twins."

"Aye," Ms. Griffin said. "Their mother said they had gone to investigate there. No one has found evidence they were there. But..." She waved her finger at me and Jade, leaned over, and spoke in a hushed voice. "Don't go over to that house again. It's haunted. You hear me? Rumors of people going in and not returning."

"Do you know its history?" Jade asked.

Ms. Griffin looked around them. The student body had thinned out. It was just us and a few scattered youths waiting for their parents. She sat down on the ledge of a nearby bleacher and leaned forward. She had told Jade and me several stories of the town since I had known her. For one, she was a history teacher, and well, I guess she liked to tell stories. And second, she loved to gossip.

"What I tell you now, don't go blathering about it. It's mostly rubbish." She stared hard down at me, and I nodded. She looked to Jade and Thomas who both confirmed they understood too.

"Long ago, there were two children who came to town. About your age, in fact. Brother and sister. Never knew what happened with the sister. The boy was named Ronan and grew up, became successful. He gave money to the town, even to help build our yonder library and town hall. It was said he tinkered in magic, too, and it was innocent enough. But there were other rumors about him. Even far stranger." She glanced over her shoulder.

Thomas had crept up and was leaning forward, knelt on one knee with his elbow resting on his leg to prop his head up. "What other bloody rumors?"

Ms. Griffin sighed. "It doesn't matter. That part is all rubbish."

"Was he a bad person?" Jade asked, moving the conversation forward.

"No, child," Ms. Griffin said. "He wasn't bad at first. But you see his wife died of cancer. Then his son and daughter passed away at sea during a storm. He despaired, and well, he used what magic he knew for dark purposes."

"Dark? What'd he do?" I asked.

"He wanted to bring his children back from the other side. It's said he opened a portal there in his house, and though he never found his children, he found a new home on the other side. It's said he comes back on occasion, and you can hear noises in that house," Ms. Griffin said.

I swallowed.

Ms. Griffin stood up and shook her head. "What I think happened is he died a lonely man. And now his wretched spirit wanders that house, and you shouldn't go near it."

Ms. Griffin sighed. "I shouldn't have told you that tale. But the point is this. Ever since Ronan's children were lost at sea, that house has been nothing but darkness. Some fellas go traipsing inside and never come out. When I was at university, I heard they found a young man, who had been inside like Brian, wandering close to the house. It was late June. When they found him wandering the street, he gave a great tale of going into a magical portal, but strangest of all, he had frostbite."

"Frostbite?" Thomas asked, poking a finger in his ear to root out any earwax. "Frostbite? How's that happen in June?"

Ms. Griffin shrugged. "That's enough. But I'll tell you children, stay away from that house."

"What was the other rumor?" I asked. "You said it was rubbish, but he was suspected to be something else? A warlock?"

Dylan's voice spoke over my head. "He was a werewolf."

I turned around, and Dylan was standing behind me.

Jade and Thomas said in unison, "Werewolf?"

Thomas slapped his forehead and rolled his eyes. "Werewolf! What the blimey—"

A low hoarse voice hollered Thomas's name across the gym. A man stood by the door wearing a gray tweed cap on his head, stubble over his face, and he waved impatiently for Thomas to come.

Thomas sighed. "Me uncle. Right when it was getting good. A werewolf living on Lowre Few Lane." He got up and said in a hushed voice to me, "Codger always has bad timing." Thomas waved to everyone. "Cheers, mates."

Ms. Griffin put her hands on her hips and gave Dylan a reproachful look. "Mr. Payne, I thought Headmaster Collins had called your aunt."

"Well," Dylan said, "my aunt is not answering any calls." He shrugged and sat down next to me, putting his arm around my shoulder. "But I'm going to stay with my homey here." He squeezed my shoulders, put his head on my arm, and then let go. I was about to faint.

Ms. Griffin wore a confused look. "Your *homey*? Mr. Payne. We use plain English here at—"

A boy and girl several feet away got into a shoving match, and Ms. Griffin sighed and shook her head. "Lord have mercy on me soul, and let this day be over..." She waltzed over to the students, barking orders.

Jade's phone rang, and she answered. "Mum. Where are you?" Her eyes opened wide, and she said, "*Where?* Mum, that's all the way in England. I tried to call you, then

Cousin Janine, and even Granny." She stuck her bottom lip out. "Oh, I didn't know that." She brought the phone away from her mouth and told us, "Granny is visiting in France, and Cousin Janine had to take her girlfriend to a hospital to deliver a baby." She brought the phone to her ear. "What'd you say, Mum? Yes, Colton is here. I'll ask him. Mum, you have no idea what I've been through—"

She furrowed her brow. "Mum?" Her eyes lit up. "Oh, there you are. Yes, I said Colton's here in front of me." She sighed, looked up at me, and asked, "Is it okay if I stay with you until Cousin Janine can pick me up?"

I nodded.

Jade said on the phone, "He said I can. Yes, I'm okay. No, I'm not injured. I promise. Okay, I'll tell you the story later then. Bye." She hung up and appeared disappointed that she didn't get to tell her story.

Dylan looked around the gym, then to me and asked, "It is okay if I stay with you too? I told Headmaster Collins we made plans, and well, my aunt is not answering." He frowned for a second, showing his concern, but then replaced it with a smile. "I heard you have a badminton set. We can play?"

My head almost fell off nodding with pure zest.

A high-pitched woman's voice cut sharply from across the other side of the gym. "*Where's me wee little scab?*"

I groaned and rolled my eyes. At the door stood a middle-aged black woman dressed in a cinnamon-colored polka-dot dress and wearing a full-brim hat on her head. Gray hair fell out from underneath to her shoulders.

"That's Georgia," I said as I got up and put my bag over a shoulder. "I warn you. She's not a full shilling, if you know what I mean."

Dylan asked Jade, "What's that mean?"

"I think you would say in America, she's a sandwich short of a picnic."

I glanced back to Dylan and smiled. "Nooo blimey idea why my parents think she's a safe child-sitter."

Dylan grinned, his dimples formed, and my head swooned. I was beyond excited he was staying with me, even if it was for a short period.

I had no idea we were heading into an adventure beyond words.

Chapter Eight

BEFORE WE HEADED out of the building to the car, Dylan and Jade introduced themselves to Georgia. Or, I should say, Georgia made her introduction; and a grand production it was.

I walked across the gym toward Georgia, dreading the certain-to-come cheek-pinching. Dylan and Jade were at my back. Georgia was a rotund woman who loved her turquoise lipstick, loved fancy colorful dresses, and must have had a hundred different hats in her closet because she always had a new one on the top of her head.

Georgia held her hand over her mouth and acted like she had not seen me for years, although I'd just seen her two weeks before for an entire weekend while my parents were away.

She bent down, pinched my cheek hard, jiggled it up and down, not letting go, and said, "How's my sweet wee scab? I haven't seen you in forever. Look at you. You sprouted up three fists, you have." She let me go and looked me up and down. "You been eating? Looking more like bone than flesh. Never mind that. I'll get a healthy meal in you." She put her hands on her hips. "Well, how are you? You going to wag your tongue and talk, or a leprechaun enchanted it to be still?"

"I'm fine," I moaned, rubbing my face.

She looked over my shoulder at Jade and Dylan, and I jabbed my thumb in their direction. "They need to stay with us until their parents can get them."

Jade waved her hand. "I'm Jade."

Georgia put a hand over her mouth, giggled, and muttered. "But you both are cute as buttons, you are. Allow me to introduce meself." She swept her hat off her head, causing her gray, coarse shoulder-length hair to flip in the air. Her charcoal eyebrows lifted up, and she made a curtsy. "Madame Georgia. But you just call me Georgia." She put her hat to her chest and leaned toward Dylan, asking, "And what's your name, young shining knight?"

Dylan glanced at me and stuck his hand out. "I'm Dylan."

Georgia ignored his hand and pinched his cheek too. "Aren't you the cutest little bugger ever. And I love your accent."

Dylan squinted from the pinch and turned beet red.

"Uh, Georgia, can you sign me out, and them too?" I pointed to a table where a teacher monitor sat.

Georgia let Dylan go, checked us out, and then put her elbow out to Jade. "I hear you had rabid beasts in your midst today?"

Jade took Georgia's arm, and we walked toward the sedan. Jade seemed excited as she finally got to tell someone about the near miss.

Dylan rubbed his cheek and looked over to me, his eyes wide. I shrugged and whispered, "I tried to warn you."

A couple of minutes later, we sat inside Georgia's sedan and were on our way to my house. Dylan and I sat in the back seat, and Jade was up in the passenger side. Georgia drove with both of her hands on the steering wheel, leaned forward, her chin barely an inch from the wheel. I sighed in relief from the cessation of Georgia's chatter.

Two things shut Madame Georgia up—driving and watching reruns of sitcoms I'm sure were popular three decades before I was born.

"Can I borrow your phone? Going to call my aunt again," Dylan said from my side.

I reached into my jacket, plucked it out from a pocket, and handed it over. "Where's yours?"

He sighed. "I think I lost it when everyone went crazy with the wolves and were running inside. It's probably out in the field. Headmaster Collins wouldn't let me look for it. Said it was too dangerous."

"Oh," I said.

Jade glanced back from her seat. Her expression was full of suspicion. Her gaze met mine.

I shrugged, confused as to why she was giving me that particular look. Did Dylan just say something to raise her suspicion? She didn't say anything, though, but turned back around.

Dylan dialed a number and put the phone up to his ear. After a few moments, he brought it down and handed it back. His lips pursed together, and he glanced between the two front seats, out the front windshield and then back to me.

"Can we stop at my house? I just want to see if my aunt's there."

I felt a tinge of disappointment. Dylan's aunt would be home, we'd have to drop him off, and it'd just be myself and Jade. I pushed this selfish thought away and nodded.

I leaned up and said, "Georgia?"

She startled and glanced over her shoulder before snapping her eyes forward again.

"What is it, lad? I'm driving, if you hadn't noticed."

"Um, can you take Dylan home? He wants to see if his aunt is there."

Georgia made one perceptible nod. "This car won't find the dwelling by itself. What's the address?"

Dylan answered. "Fifty Lowre Few Lane."

Georgia looked up into the rearview mirror and back down to the road. "You live o'er there? Not many folks out there anymore. Not to mention there's that house everyone knows is haunted. Well, you're just a cherub. Not like you choose where you live."

Several minutes later, we pulled down Lowre Few Lane. Number 44 was on Dylan's side, and I stared past him and noticed his gaze was fixed on it too.

Georgia asked me about the number of wolves we'd seen, distracting me, and I answered. The house was behind us by then, but something had been different about the place. I couldn't put my finger on it.

Georgia pulled up into Dylan's driveway and stopped. "We'll wait right here."

Dylan emanated an air of unease as he opened the door. "Thank you." Before he shut his door, he gave me a small wave and half smile, and then he ran to his front door and disappeared inside.

Georgia hunched over the steering wheel, stared out of the windshield, and muttered, "Feels like we're anywhere but Ireland, don't it? You think they send a bus out here? I suppose they do. And that scary house over yonder as your neighbor. Gives me the willies, it does."

Dylan came back out, locked the door, and ran to the car. A frown was etched over his face.

Georgia rolled her window down. "What is it, lad?"

Dylan shook his head. "She's not home."

"You leave her a note?" Georgia asked.

Dylan nodded.

"Get in then. You can wait at the house for her to phone. She probably went to get some groceries and wandered from there. It happens to me all the time. She'll be back shortly."

Dylan got in, and we backed out and drove back in the direction we'd come. The old house was now on my side, and I stared at it. A chill wound its way up my spine, and I swallowed hard.

One of the wolf statues that had been at the bottom of the porch had been moved. It was on the porch, set near the front door. And rather than sitting, it was now standing.

I looked over to Dylan. He was not paying any attention to the house, though. My jaw bobbed up and down. "T-the house..."

He rubbed his hands on his knees over and over and looked over to me. "What?"

I shook my head. "Nothing."

A few minutes later, Georgia pulled into my neighborhood and said from the front, "All our driving around has made me absolutely zonked. I'll not be cooking up my roasted chicken casserole and crumpets for you tonight."

I breathed a silent thank-you. Georgia's cooking was akin to eating lumps of rocks.

"It goes against my better nature, it does," Georgia said, "but we can order out. What do you all want?"

I opened my mouth, but Georgia glanced up in the rearview mirror and wagged her finger, cutting me short. "Not that slimy, cheesy stuff either."

Dylan looked away from his window, a smile forming on his face. "Pizza?"

Georgia shook her head. "Aye. Not a proper meal."

"Supermac's," Jade suggested.

Georgia complained about that, too, and I suggested Japanese. That caused an uproar.

Georgia went on about spending five pounds on a bit of fish meat. "I could take you all to the Irish Sea, and we could catch us a bucket-load of fish..."

In the end, Supermac's was what she ordered. I had no idea how it differed from greasy pizza. Georgia parked the car and stepped inside the house, saying she had to use the restroom.

Jade, Dylan, and I stood in my driveway near the car.

After the door closed, Jade wheeled to Dylan and put her hands on her hips. "Something is not brewing right. Tell us what's going on."

"What?" Dylan asked, scratching the back of his neck. He looked down the street. "You have a lot of neighbors."

Jade pointed her finger at him. "You're not telling the truth."

Dylan looked between her and me. "I'm shooting straight. Swear."

Jade shook her head. "I don't know what that means. But you said you lost your phone when you were running inside with everyone."

"So?" Dylan said.

She poked his chest. "But you told Ms. Griffin and Headmaster Collins you were in the loo when we were attacked by wolves. You can't be in two places at once. So which was it?"

"Oh. Well—" Dylan said, his eyes widened.

"Yeah," I said, interrupting. A new realization came to me. I squared myself off to him. "And I heard you calling my name when I was running toward Jade."

Dylan licked his upper lip. "Oh, that—"

I did not let him get a word in edgewise. "And I heard you quarreling with your aunt last night. It sounded like you both have been fibbing to everyone." I pointed my finger at him. "And when you came to the gym, you were in complete flitters. Why did you take your shoes off in the first place? And you had long black hair all over you."

Dylan stared down at the ground and pushed both of his hands through his hair. "You got me." He sighed and rubbed his forehead with one hand. "Oh man, my aunt is going to go ballistic if she finds out I told you this. I've never told anyone about this part of me. You're not going to believe this."

Jade cocked her head to the side. "You being gay doesn't explain all the fibs, Dylan. So try again, sir."

"What?" Dylan's blush deepened a bit more. "I mean. Oh, wow. Do other people know?"

"You're gay?" I asked, clapping my hands.

Jade punched my arm. I grimaced and rubbed where she hit.

Jade shook her head. "Oh, darling. In your house, I saw you had a love letter from Sebastian. Says he thinks of you every night."

"Who's Sebastian?" I asked, my voice rising. I looked to Jade. "You never told me about the letter."

Dylan answered. "Some boy I know in Portland. He likes to write letters rather than emails or texts. Go figure." Dylan furrowed his brow. "And you shouldn't be going through people's stuff."

"And," Jade said, "you shouldn't leave it on the back of the toilet for everyone to see." She looked to me. "I didn't tell you because it wasn't your business." Jade returned her gaze to Dylan and wagged her finger. "Don't change the subject, Dylan. That little detail doesn't explain all this fibbery."

Dylan sighed. "That was not what I was going to say. You see, my aunt, she's a witch."

I glanced to Dylan and then to Jade. *Did I just hear him right?* Jade's mouth popped open.

Dylan pulled his hair up with both hands. "But that's not all. That black wolf you saw today. That was me." He offered a sheepish grin. "I'm a werewolf."

This time, my jaw dropped to the ground.

Chapter Nine

A WHOLE NUMBING five minutes had passed since Dylan's disclosure. I'd sat down on the edge of the driveway and pulled my knees up to my chest.

During the awkward interval, Jade asked the same two questions with slight differences each time.

"Did you just say you're a werewolf?"

"Yes."

"Like a real werewolf you see in the pictures?"

"Pictures? Oh, the movies. Yes."

"And your aunt's a witch?"

"Yes."

"You're saying you can change to a wolf and then back?"

"Yes."

"Do it now?"

"Well, I'm not supposed to. And it'd be, uh, improper. I have to take off my clothes."

"So you don't like garlic or silver bullets?"

"Um, well, any bullets are bad news. A little silver is fine, but too much and I get weak knees. And garlic deals with vampires and has nothing to do with werewolves."

"Your aunt makes brews and spells?"

"I guess. Probably."

"She rides a broom at night?"

"I don't think so. Just seen her sweep with one."

Dylan sat down several feet away from me on the driveway. He played with some pebbles on the ground. Jade stood in the middle of the driveway, twiddled her hair with one finger, and stared at Dylan with large, terrified eyes.

A thought hit me, and I snapped my gaze over to Dylan. "So you weren't in the loo today. You saved us."

Jade glanced from me to Dylan. Her finger quit spinning her hair as she waited for him to answer.

Dylan chuckled. "Took you long enough. Yes."

I thrust my finger in the air. "And you were at the house that day Jade and I were there."

Dylan gave one nod.

"What were those white wolves?" I asked.

Dylan shrugged. "Don't know."

The bushes close to the house rustled, and there was a loud noise. "*Achoo! Achoo!*"

Jade screeched, forgot her fear of Dylan, and ran behind him. I leaped to my feet, grabbed a croquet mallet that had been left in the yard, and backed toward Dylan, my weapon raised over my head.

Dylan was the only one not alarmed. "I think it's your red-haired friend."

I gave Dylan a quizzical glance and looked back to the bushes. "Thomas?"

Thomas's messy red hair popped out from the top of the bush, and he stared out at us. He stumbled from the foliage with a leaf in his mouth, one stuck to the end of his nose, and a couple of others plastered to a cheek. He spat out one and plucked the others away. One leaf stuck to his fingers, and he flapped his hand about, trying to dislodge it.

"Thomas!" Jade cried out. "What are you doing here?"

Thomas picked twigs out from his hair. "What's it blimey well look like I'm doing? I'm joining in on your adventure."

"What adventure, you clonk?" I asked.

He pointed to Dylan. "When I heard 44 Lowre Few Lane, I knew something spectacular was going to happen." He wagged his finger at Dylan. "And now I hear he's a werewolf. This is bloody fantastic."

"*Thomas*," Jade said, "Where's your uncle?"

"Oh, him," Thomas said and waved his hand in dismissal. "I told me gormless uncle to drop me off at the mall."

"The mall?" Jade asked. "It's twelve kilometers away! You're nowhere close."

"Aye," Thomas said and honked out laughter. "Me uncle barely knows which way is up, let alone where the mall is. He dropped me off a kilometer up the way." He held up some coins in his hand. "I used my bus tokens to get here."

"So, why were you hiding, dude?" Dylan asked.

Thomas shrugged. "I started to wait over yonder but fell asleep. Where were you anyway? Took you all long enough."

"Thomas, what makes you think we're going on an adventure?" Jade questioned.

Thomas puffed his chest out and looked proud to know something we didn't. "After I left, I thought of something my uncle once told me. I already told you he said there was some kind of door inside. But I remembered he said it led to a world of snow and ice," he whispered. "I thought he was telling a tall tale. But I'm thinking he might have seen inside the place."

I put my hands on my hips. "Thomas O'Leary, what else do you know about this house at 44 Lowre Few Lane? If you have answers, spill them now."

Thomas's animation died, and he stared down at the ground in shame. "Don't know bloody much else. Just that Lowre Few spells werewolf."

"*What?*" I glanced at Jade.

Jade spoke in a breathless tone. "Lowre Few spells werewolf?" Her head swiveled back, and she focused upward with one finger raised, swirling it in the air. She appeared to be unscrambling the words in her head.

I glanced over to Dylan. He stuck his bottom lip out, brought up both hands, and shrugged.

I mentally broke down the anagram *Lowre Few* in my mind, worked it out, and said with awe, "Blimey sake, it does."

Thomas looked back up with a sheepish look. "I know it's not much. But anything called Werewolf Lane with a haunted house and a doorway to an icy world has to mean something grand, right?"

"Thomas," I said, "did someone tell you that Lowre Few spelled werewolf?"

He shook his head and stared at all of us. "No. Why? Someone supposed to?"

"No," I muttered. Thomas sometimes did stuff like this that took me completely by surprise.

"What's all this mean?" Thomas asked.

"That," Jade said, "is a good question. Hmm, I wonder who could give us answers."

Thomas, Jade, and I turned to Dylan. Each of us crossed our arms, and tapped one foot up and down, waiting for him to talk.

"Uh," Dylan said. He gave a crooked smile and pushed his bangs out his eyes. "Wha's up?"

Jade's eyes narrowed. "For starters, how'd you know our *red-haired* friend was in the bushes?"

"Oh." Dylan chuckled. "Really awesome sense of smell." He looked to Thomas. "No offense. I'm, uh, you know...part canine."

Thomas hooted out laughter and clapped his hands. "That's brilliant. I think I had gas anyway." He looked over at me and Jade, a huge grin plastered on his face. When he noticed we had frowns on ours, his smile vanished. He stared hard at Dylan again, recrossed his arms over his chest, and tapped his foot up and down in sync with ours.

Jade swirled one finger in the air and asked, "Dylan, tell us, what's your story?"

Dylan coughed into his hand. "Okay, well, you want the short or long?" He looked at everyone, and no one answered. "Let's try the short version. I was living in Portland. And I was changing into a werewolf at weird times. My parents sent me here to my aunt so she could help me."

I glanced to Jade and Thomas who both had bewildered looks. "Is that it?" I asked.

Dylan smiled nervously and squirmed. "Okay, first. Only a few people in the family line have been werewolves, so my family and I have been on our own. But sometimes when you're a werewolf youth around the age of twelve or thirteen, you start, uh, changing and stuff. Things happen to your body, and you don't have control over it. Well, you know what I'm saying, right?"

I shook my head and so did Jade and Thomas.

Dylan laughed. "Oh, right, I guess you wouldn't. Well, sometimes the changes come at really awkward times."

Thomas pulled on his ears, biting his lip. "For one moment there, I thought I knew what you're talking about. But I'm lost."

Dylan massaged his face and uttered, "This is much harder to explain than I thought." He held his finger up. "Okay. This was the problem. I was changing all the time into a werewolf. Several times at night, in the morning before I went to school, and sometimes, while I was at school. Luckily, I felt the changes and made it somewhere isolated. Once, I locked myself up in the toilet stall until my dad picked me up. The point being, I had no self-control. So, my parents sent me here to be with my aunt, who is a witch and could help me control my changes." He sighed.

"Ohhh," Jade said. "So you have been learning to control yourself since June?"

I snapped my fingers. "And you just learned how to do it recently? Your aunt wanted you to start school to see if you could keep it under control."

Dylan nodded and gestured like he was shooting a gun with his hand. "Bingo. And now I'm super wicked good at it. Can change on a dime and back. It's really cool. My aunt wants me to stay with her for the year, though, to make sure everything is good. And she said I am not supposed to change unless I ask permission."

"So you never went to a boarding school?" I asked.

Dylan shook his head. "No. Sorry I lied. We didn't know what else to say. It'd be kinda weird to tell people you've been learning self-control over your werewolf powers."

Thomas nodded. "Aye, that sure is not something you hear every day."

"That night I saw you at that old house? What were you doing?" I asked.

"Well, one day, Erin was walking to her uncle's who had been visiting. I walked with her. We came across that house. And she dared me to go up to the porch and touch a wolf statue. I said I would do it if she would. We both ran up, touched a statue, and ran back. We were laughing and going up the hill when I heard a noise back at the house. Erin didn't hear, just me. I didn't think much about it. But ever since then, everyone has been hearing noises at the house. I go investigate in my wolf form. It, you know, feels safer. Please don't tell my aunt."

"Have you gone inside the house?" Jade asked.

Dylan emphatically shook his head. "No, no, no. For one, I'd be in big trouble if she knew I was snooping around outside. But if she found out I had gone inside…" He pretended to wipe sweat from his brow. "Whew. It wouldn't be pretty."

"Do you know what happened to the Kennedy twins?" I asked.

"No." Dylan scratched the back of his neck and frowned. "But my aunt was talking nonsense last night about this Ronan character Ms. Griffin mentioned. It didn't make a whole lot of sense."

Jade leaned in. "Ronan. The one Ms. Griffin says knows magic?"

Dylan shrugged. "I guess. That's what she says."

"And a werewolf?" I added.

Dylan put his hands up. "That's what my aunt said."

"Well, what else did your aunt say?" I pressed.

"She was packing some clothes and told me to go to bed, but then she called someone. I think my parents. She said Ronan was back. Said something about kidnapping. I got worried, too, because I think she said something about sending me back. Then she came to the door where I was eavesdropping and pointed to my room, so I went to bed. That's all I heard. She got me up early this morning for my rugby practice. We've been practicing before dawn. She had a suitcase and told me she had to drop clothes off for a family several miles away, and she'd see me after school."

"Do you think she dropped off the clothes?" Jade asked.

Dylan messed his hair, and that worry was back in his expression. "I don't know. I didn't think anything of it. But I remembered something after I saw those white wolves."

"What?" I asked.

"Well," Dylan said, "she was packing winter clothes. Coats and gloves and stuff."

Chapter Ten

A FEW MINUTES later, the fast-food Supermac's delivery car pulled up into the drive. A young woman with a ponytail got out, holding a large brown paper bag in one hand.

I started to the house and told everyone, "I'll get some money."

Georgia was already walking out the front door, though. She came down the porch steps and looked over to Thomas. "Is me eyes deceiving me, or are you all multiplying?"

"Oh," I said. "This is just Thomas. Uh, his uncle had something to do and dropped him off."

She stopped in front of Thomas. His wide grin faltered as she leaned forward and pinched his cheek.

"Look at you, lad. Let's get some meat on those bones." She let him go and raised her eyeglasses up from her nose, inspecting his hair. "Will you look at that red. You have a mess of it, too, don't you?"

Thomas snickered, his face turning as crimson as his hair, and he stared down with an awkward smile.

She stepped over to the delivery person and said over her shoulder, "Well, hope you're staying for dinner. Me stomach is tossing side to side like a ship on a stormy sea. Not going to be eating anything for a long time. Probably those doughnuts I had for lunch." She paid the girl and waved us all inside.

Georgia had us sit down at the dinner table, making us eat our fast food meal off my mother's nice plates.

She made certain we had napkins, silverware that lay uselessly by the side of our plates, and glasses of water, and then she started toward the living room.

"After supper, you're to stay in the house. Telly says there's more dog packs running around outside. Some are saying they're wolves." She shook her head. "Where would wolves come from?"

She continued to the living room, mumbling, but stopped in midstep to turn to us once again. "You know some lass named Erin Clarke?"

I exchanged looks with everyone.

"Yes, ma'am. Why?" Jade said.

Georgia sighed. "Lass has gone missing. No one knows where she went." She pointed her finger toward me. "And your dad phoned me and said he can't get back tonight, and you're to stay put. No dance."

"It was cancelled, ma'am," Jade said.

"Well, good," Georgia said, and her gaze roved over everyone else at the table. "Listen carefully. You're all to stay here until your family comes to get you." She waggled her finger and said, "I'll have you all flogged if you don't mind."

"Yes, ma'am," each of us responded one by one.

Georgia walked into the living room, sat down hard on the couch, and pointed the remote control at the TV to turn the volume up. I turned back to everyone. Dylan and Jade caught my stare. Thomas was the only one oblivious, wolfing down his cheeseburger and gobbling his fries. I started to eat, but my hunger had taken a nosedive.

"Dylan, what's going on?" I asked in a hushed voice.

"I don't know," he said around a bite of fried potatoes.

Jade was on her smartphone. "I'm calling Erin." She let her phone ring and then frowned and put it down. "No answer." She tapped her screen. "Going to see what news stories are out."

"Told you, Colton," Thomas said across from me.

I looked over at him, and he was pointing into the living room at the television.

I stared at the TV where the meteorological person was speaking. "An understatement, but this is quite unusual weather."

I got up from my chair and stepped closer. Georgia leaned her head back against the couch cushion, and snores poured from her mouth.

The weatherman said, "In the last few hours, the temperature has dropped another five degrees in what meteorologists are describing as one of the rarest phenomena of the twenty-first century. This drop in temperature is not due to any normal activity of a low-pressure system colliding with a high-pressure system. This storm is only actually affecting the city of Arklow. You heard me right. Other cities on the coast of Ireland are not being affected."

I glanced toward the dinner table. Dylan and Thomas were staring with large eyes at the TV. Jade was tapping on her phone and not paying attention.

The weatherman continued his piece. "A team from the World Meteorological Organization has been dispatched to the region to investigate—"

"Look at this," Jade said, interrupting the rather disturbing news story on TV.

"*Jade*," I said, staring over at her. "Aren't you even watching this?"

Jade was indeed not watching the TV since her gaze was fixed on her smartphone. She waved her hand at me and said, "Never mind the blooming TV. Look at this!"

"What?" I strode over to her.

She handed the phone to Dylan. He looked down at it, placed his finger on the screen, and scrolled down.

I flailed my hands. "Well? What could be more bloody interesting than this?"

Dylan continued to read whatever was on the screen. He scrolled down and finally looked up at me and swallowed. He handed me the smartphone. I lifted it and discovered the content was not even related to the current day. It was a news story about the local library of Arklow, or really about a seminar that they had held over the last year about tales from the past. One was a short story Jade had singled out with the heading: *Baron Ronan Karl Loses Family in Sea, Then Goes Crazy.*

I opened my eyes wide and said, "He lived a long time ago. In the late 1800s." Then I read the story aloud. "Ronan tragically lost his daughter and son when they were on a ferry boat traveling from England. The bodies were never retrieved, but Ronan made plots in his back lot, then became a hermit. This would have been the end of a catastrophic tale, except a year later an old friend happened by Ronan's home and would later tell a grim tale. The friend recalled that the entire street of Lowre Few Lane had vacated. He learned that the neighbors, who had been relations to one degree or another, had become fearful of Ronan and fled.

"Ronan had always been known to perform magic tricks for local children. The friend said Ronan had become delusional, and he was convinced he was a sorcerer and traveled back and forth to another world with the intent to bring his children back to life. The friend, at that point, fled the home."

I shook my head. "Well, it's interesting. But why do you think this is so blimey important?"

Jade smacked her forehead. "Did you even see the photograph below the story?"

"The photograph?"

I scrolled down to the bottom, and there was a black-and-white photo of Ronan standing behind what was most likely his son and daughter. The children looked to be about my age. I peered closer at the screen and my breath caught. The girl had blonde curly hair, was grinning, and had a large gap between her front teeth.

"T-that looks like—"

"Erin," Jade said.

"Look at the son," Dylan said.

I did. The son was very handsome, had large dark locks of hair that hung in front of his face and dimples on his cheeks. I turned my gaze up to Dylan. "He looks exactly like you."

Thomas came to my side and pulled on my arm so he could see the phone.

I absent-mindedly handed it over, then sat down next to Dylan. "So, your family is from here. Your aunt said he's a werewolf. So it's not a leap of logic to think he may be old family. You're probably related."

"Well, Aunt Ruth did once tell me I was related to someone who used to live in the house. But then she didn't say any more. I think she let that slip by accident." Dylan stroked his chin and asked, "But Erin too?"

"Right, she did tell me she thought she had family long ago who lived on Lowre Few Lane. It's why she was curious about that house." A nervous chuckle erupted from Jade, and she shook her head. "But she has never mentioned being a werewolf. I think I'd remember that conversation."

"Like I said. Not every child born in the family can turn into a wolf. In fact, as far as I know, only a couple of distant relatives can do it. Most are lucky normal human kids," Dylan said.

Thomas stared down at Dylan and hooted laughter. "Lucky to be a regular bloke? I'd love to be a werewolf. I'd have me a queue of lasses, each waiting to give me a snog."

Dylan furrowed his brow and grinned. "A snog?"

"Kiss," I said.

"Oh," Dylan said and chuckled. "I guess some of it's cool. But it's not all it sounds. You can have issues with fleas that don't go away even after you change back. Sometimes a rare steak sounds better than a cooked one. Plus you never know when you might change, and trust me, that's stressful. It's a curse."

I hadn't realized that being a werewolf meant so many complications. Dylan was like me in some ways. I was one of the few Asians in my school, which came with its challenges of being considered "smart" or being ignored. I was actually a decent tennis player, but I never got any playing time.

Jade's phone buzzed on the table in front of me, and the ringtone of barking dogs brayed out.

I sighed. "Really, Jade? Given everything that has happened, can't you find a new ringtone?"

I looked at the caller ID and drew in a breath. "*Oh, bloody turds!*"

Jade held her hand out. "Who is it?"

I handed the phone over. She snatched it from my hand and stared at the caller ID. Her mouth dropped, and she put the phone up to her head. "H-hello?"

"Who is it?" Dylan asked.

I licked my top lip and said, "It's Erin."

Chapter Eleven

JADE HELD THE phone up to her ear. Her knuckles were white from gripping the phone hard. She stood rigid, her face pale, and stammered, "E-Erin? Is that you?"

Thomas, Dylan, and I huddled together and leaned close, trying to catch what was being said on the other end of the line. The noise from the TV in the adjacent room was breaking my concentration, and I could barely make out Erin's strained voice on the line.

"W-what?" Jade said, her voice shaking. "Where did you say? You're breaking up."

"What's she saying?" Thomas asked, pulling on his hair with both hands.

Jade cut Thomas a sharp look. She shoved her palm up in the air to quiet him, her brow furrowed, and half turned away from us.

"White wolves? Where are you? Erin?" Jade's eyes were jumbo size, and her mouth opened and closed. She whispered, "Who's coming? Erin?"

A sharp scream came from the other end, and Jade flinched, pulling the phone away from her ear. She put it back to her head. "*Erin! You there? Erin?*" Jade stared down at the screen. "She hung up."

Jade touched her screen again. She tapped her fingers, then brought it up to her ear. A second later, she yanked it from the side of her head. The loud screech was pronounced.

Jade hung up the call, put the phone on the dinner table, and stared vacantly.

Dylan coughed into his hand, and his voice sounded spooked. "So Erin's in trouble?"

Jade gave a barely perceptible nod but didn't speak. Her eyelids fluttered up and down.

Thomas whispered in my ear. "I believe a light is running upstairs, but no one's home."

I elbowed Thomas, then snapped my fingers in front of her face. "Jade?"

She startled and stared at me.

"What did Erin say?"

"S-she was kidnapped, I think. S-she saw an ice castle."

Dylan spoke in a dubious tone and shook his head. "Ice castle? What does that mean?"

Thomas shook his head and spoke with a squeak. "They got her up in the North Pole!"

"Wait. Jade, is that the name of the place?" I took my phone out and completed a search for a place called Ice Castle. There was a restaurant in London called that.

"No." She looked up and met my gaze. "No. I mean Erin was kidnapped and taken t-to 44 Lowre Few Lane. I think she managed to get away and was hiding inside the house somewhere. She said she was close to the front door and there was a magical doorway near her..." Jade patted her cheeks with both hands. "On the other side of this door, she could see an ice castle. Then that's it."

"A magical doorway. An ice castle. Erin was taken to Ronan's world," I said.

Dylan muttered, "That's where Aunt Ruth must have went..."

We all looked up, and Dylan was staring out the dining room window.

"What?" I asked.

"My aunt," Dylan said. "Obviously, she went into that house, and she's over there in another world. That's why she was packing a coat and gloves. She went over to get those Kennedy boys. She must have found one." He turned to me, his eyes opened wide, then looked everyone over. "You said one of the Kennedy brothers was in the hospital now not far from my house?"

Jade nodded. "Yes."

"Well," Dylan said, his voice rising. "Don't you see? Aunt Ruth saved one brother. But she's still over there. Maybe looking for the other or maybe trapped. Now, Erin is there too. *We need to go save them.*"

I wrung my hands and glanced at Georgia on the couch. Snores poured rhythmically from her mouth. "W-we should call the coppers. We're not supposed to leave."

Thomas put his hands in the air. "You know I've never been accused of being the brains, but when you ring the plods, what're you going to say?" He gestured having a phone up to his ear. "Yes, sir. Send some coppers over to 44 Lowre Few Lane. There's a man who we believe to be a werewolf and magician. He used to live at the house in the late 1800s, and we think he still does. But one other wee detail. He does not really live in the house, you see. He lives in another world made of ice; you just need to get into the house and figure out how to get over into his world through some dodgy magical portal. Oh, it's no problem, sir. You're welcome. Good luck in finding him and cheers."

"Thomas has a point," Jade said.

I swallowed and barely gave one perceptible nod. "What are we going to do then?"

Dylan tapped his chin and asked Thomas, "How many bus tokens you have left?"

Thomas poked his hand into his pocket, brought his hand up, and opened it. There were four tokens lying on his palm.

Dylan grinned and slapped his shoulder. "You're totally off the hook, dude!"

Thomas bawled out, "Brilliant!"

Dylan asked Jade if she could call the hospital and see if she could find out if the brother was awake. Jade asked how she was supposed to do that.

Thomas leaned over to me and whispered, "Colton, what's 'off the hook' mean?"

"Um, I think it means, uh..." I scratched my head and finally shook my head. "No idea. But it's a good thing."

Thomas grinned and said in a quiet voice, "Off the hook."

"Look." Dylan pointed into the living room at the TV.

The local news was on. The camera showed a picture of a young man lying in bed, a couple of IVs stuck in his arm, and his mother by his side. The caption read *Brian Kennedy awakens after mysterious disappearance. Brother David Kennedy remains missing.*

I squeaked. "He's awake."

"Guys," Dylan said, "We have to go see him. He might be able to tell us something useful." He hopped up and down. "Come on, let's go."

"Wait," Jade said.

"*What?*" Dylan was bursting at the seams to depart.

Jade pointed down the hall, toward my room, asking me, "You have some mittens and stocking hats? We might need them."

Several minutes later, we stood at the front door. Everyone had their backpack on their shoulders; packed in them was heavier clothing. I looked at Georgia where she slept on the couch.

A sharp snort spurted from her mouth, and she mumbled, "I'll get that chicken, Granny. Don't you worry."

I glanced at everyone then stopped to stare at Dylan.

He offered a half smile and said in a quiet voice. "Come on, bro, let's go."

"Wait." I held my finger up, then walked into the kitchen, took out a notepad and pen, and wrote a note.

Dear Ms. Georgia,

We have gone over to Dylan's home to grab something he lost. We will be back home very soon. I have my phone.

Colton

I put the note on the table and stepped over to everyone. "Let's go."

Thomas pumped his fist in the air. "Off the hook!"

Dylan gave Thomas an uncertain look and shook his head. "No, dude. That's just bad timing." He patted Thomas's arm. "I'll tell you when to say it."

We stepped through the front door. It was colder outside than it had been a half hour ago.

Chapter Twelve

WE SAT IN the front part of the bus as it approached our stop, a block away from the hospital. Luckily, Brian Kennedy had not been sent to the main medical center several kilometers away. Earlier reports had said he was supposed to be transported to that medical center the next day. But as luck had it, Lowre Few Lane was less than six blocks away.

The bus stopped, and the driver opened the door. He looked in the rearview mirror as we got off and told us, "The strangest weather I've seen since I was a tyke. You got any more clothes than what you're wearing? You will all turn into popsicles if you're not careful."

Jade walked down the bus steps to the curb where Dylan and Thomas were and answered him, "Yes, sir." She patted the bag over her shoulder. "We came prepared."

"Aye, that's blimey good thinking," the bus driver said and gave us a farewell wave. "Well, no telling what the evening will bring. Before you know it, there'll be a blizzard, and I'll have to hire a team of sled dogs to haul everyone around." He cackled and then flapped his hand at us as if that was the most ridiculous thought ever. He closed the door, and the bus rumbled away a second later.

We were on a street with a few businesses on one side; the hospital was in sight. The temperature had indeed dropped severely, and I was shivering. I was the first to remove my backpack and take out my warm coat, which I had not planned to wear until fall. Thomas and Jade took off their backpacks, too, and took out jackets they had borrowed from me. Thomas's outer garment hung loosely on his shoulders, and I could barely see his hands. Nothing I owned fit Thomas, so I had retrieved an old coat that had been my mum's.

"This way." Jade looked both ways and crossed the street, passing a local tavern called O'Malley's Pub. I looked through the window and was surprised to see so many patrons. Several people were pointing out of the window. Something wet and cold touched my cheek. Thomas hooted out laughter, and I wheeled around to discover large snowflakes twirling down from the sky.

A small grin formed on Dylan's face. A large flake landed on his eyelash, and I couldn't help but stare. He held his tongue out, catching the flakes, then turned to me and laughed. I smiled. Jade and Thomas held their hands out and were doing the same, catching flakes on their tongues.

The snow grew in intensity, and Dylan's smile turned downward all of a sudden. I frowned, too, as I realized this had to be tied to 44 Lowre Few.

"Oy, we should go," I said. Jade and Thomas looked to me, and realization dawned on their faces as well. Jade pursed her lips together and nodded.

Ten minutes later, we hurried into the hospital lobby, and I headed to the registration desk where an elderly woman with gray hair done up in a double-bun, wearing thick-rimmed glasses, was staring at a TV fastened to the wall. A strong scent of peach perfume wafted from her. She was watching a sitcom that Georgia liked to watch.

Dylan was at my side as we approached the desk and leaned up against it. Thomas and Jade stood behind us. The woman did not appear to hear us, but made a cursory glance and did a double take.

She shifted in her chair and said, "Oh, dear." She raised her glasses an inch off her nose and peered down at us.

"Yes, may I help you?"

"Look at her lug holes," Thomas whispered.

Dylan looked back at Thomas, confused. "Lug holes?"

"You call them ears," I whispered.

Dylan turned around to look. She did have large ears, and each had dangly earrings with a wolf that twirled as she moved.

"We're here to see Brian Kennedy," Jade announced.

She raised her eyebrows. "I see. You're family?"

Dylan nodded, coughed into his hand, and spoke—to my shock—in a feigned Irish accent. "Yes, mum. We all have had such collywobblers as me brother was found close to that creepy house on 44 Lowre Few Lane. It's such a jammy he's awake now. We're all so grateful." Dylan offered his best winning grin, cute dimples in plain view.

The woman continued to hold her glasses up as she stared at Dylan. She looked over my shoulder to Thomas, then Jade, but stopped on me.

"And you're family too?" she asked.

Jade came up to my side, gave me a one-armed hug, and leaned her head onto my shoulder. "He was adopted."

The woman sighed, let her glasses down, and fumbled with some papers on her desk. "Room 415." She leaned her elbows on her desk, and stared out at us with a hard expression. "Tell me. What do you bits know about this house on 44 Lowre Few Lane?"

Thomas opened his mouth, and my hand rose fast and sealed over it. God only knew what he was about to say. I had no doubt the word *werewolf* was going to be included.

Jade answered, "Nothing, ma'am."

The old woman tapped her gnarly fingernails on the desk, and the lines in her forehead became even more pronounced. "Nothing? Nothing at all?"

I put my hand up. "Just that it's haunted by an evil spirit named Ronan."

The elder woman regarded me, her lips pressed together. Her face turned a deep shade of red. Her gaze turned to Dylan, and she pushed her glasses up on her nose and didn't speak. Dylan stepped back into me, and I'd be lying if I said I didn't enjoy that closeness.

The woman peered over our heads; her eyes grew distant, her face softened, and she spoke with an aloof voice.

"An evil spirit, you say? That boy upstairs you seek. He spoke of an evil sorcerer living in a desolate ice land. Probably the same as your evil spirit. Living alone in ice. That doesn't sound like much of a life, does it? Living your days in a land with nothing but wind and ice?" Her stare came back down and fell on me.

I swallowed, grabbed Dylan's wrist, gave him a tug, and bumped my shoulder into Jade. "Thank you, ma'am. We'd better go upstairs."

We stepped around the desk, and I glanced back to the woman, who kept her eyes fixed on us. Thomas continued to make furtive glances toward her, his bottom lip trembling. Once in the hallway, the front desk no longer in view, we came to the elevator, and I pushed the button.

No one spoke. A ding sounded, and a woman with red hair walked out and stepped past us as the doors opened.

A man had his arm around her shoulders, telling her, "Don't worry. Brian will be more himself tomorrow."

She shook her head. "He sounds so deranged. A castle made of ice? Dark sorcerer? Werewolf? I just want to find David, and then we can worry about getting him help..."

The elevator door closed once we were inside. That had to be Brian's mom.

I tapped the fourth-floor button. "That old woman was a tad loony."

"Uh," Thomas said, "a smidge more than a tad."

Jade breathed in. "I'm just glad we're not under her gaze anymore."

Dylan twiddled with the locks over his forehead, his eyes glazed. "That perfume. There was something under it I recognized. I can almost put my finger on it."

The door dinged, and I stepped out first. There was a nurse station in front of me, but no one was manning it. I looked both ways.

Thomas bolted left, and I called out, "Thomas! Where you going?"

He spoke over his shoulder. "To Brian Kennedy's room o'course!"

Jade pointed to the wall that read 400-420 with an arrow pointing in the direction Thomas had taken.

I glanced to Dylan and Jade and dryly observed, "It ever seem to you that Thomas just likes to pretend he's a clonk?"

Jade opened her mouth, but there was a yelp far down the hall. Her eyes opened wide, and her mouth snapped closed. Dylan was the first to hurry forward and rounded a corner where Thomas had gone. I was right behind him and froze once I'd turned the corner. Jade stumbled into me.

"Colton, what are—" She stopped and stared ahead.

Thomas had fallen on his butt.

Brian Kennedy stood in the middle of the hallway, wearing his hospital gown. He gripped the mobile IV stand in front of him, staring at us, and asked in a hoarse voice, "What are you urchins doing here? This is not a nursery school, you know."

Jade stepped up. "Brian? We don't have much time. We're here to help find your brother. We know about Ronan and that he's a werewolf, among other things."

Brian's dubious expression changed, and his eyes softened. "She said you would come. She said the charms talk to her," he whispered.

"Charms?" Thomas shook his head, appearing spooked.

"Brian, what are you doing out of your bed?"

He looked at me, his eyes large. "I heard him calling."

"Who?" Dylan asked.

"David. We were walking together, near that castle. The ice spiders. They attacked, and we ran. We got split up, and I heard him calling my name. S-some lady found me. Hauled me to that door we couldn't get back to, and I was back in that house. She gave me something."

"What'd the lady look like who saved you?" Dylan asked, stepping up closer.

Brian stared vacantly forward. No one moved.

Thomas nudged me and whispered, "Methinks the captain abandoned the helm."

I stepped forward, took Brian's hand, and said, "Come on, fella. Tell us about it in your room."

Brian allowed me to take him back to his room and get him onto his bed to lie down. Then he looked at each one of us again and asked, "Who are you again?"

"Colton."

"Jade."

"Dylan."

I elbowed Thomas. "Ouch," he said, looking over at me. I twirled my finger in the air. "Oh, I'm Thomas."

Brian sat up, stared at Dylan, and said, *"You're him."*

"Who?" I asked, looking at Dylan.

"I recognize you. Your picture was everywhere in that maze where I got lost. And some girl." He reached over to his nightstand and fumbled at his wallet.

Dylan picked it up and handed it to him. Brian pushed his fingers in a side compartment. "Told me mum I wanted to keep this by my side. She thinks I'm completely off me nut."

He removed a gold coin from inside. I leaned forward to inspect it closer. Aunt Ruth had pulled a similar coin from her hutch.

"The lady told me to give this to you. Calls it a charm. Said she knew you would come see me." He handed it to Dylan. "She told me something else." Brian tapped his head. "I think she said all the bearer needs to do is make his desire known and say it out loud."

"What?" Jade asked.

"Who gave you that?" Dylan stepped in front of Jade, his hands forming fists.

I interrupted and told everyone what I had seen that night when Aunt Ruth had taken gold coins down from the top of her hutch.

"You see a girl named Erin?" Jade asked.

Brian didn't answer but stared up at the ceiling. He didn't appear to have heard Jade. "We went into the house. Set up our equipment. And then it happened, by the kitchen. A-a hole appeared. But it was more like a window, and I was staring out into an icy world. It let out on top of a temple with a large maze at the base. In the distance was a castle. Someone was about to come through, and we hid.

"A pack of white wolves ran through the hole. The front door just opened on its own, and they were about to walk out. Wish they would have, and David and I would have followed them out a minute later. We'd probably have kept running until we were to the Irish Sea. But two wolves turned toward us, and David and I ran for it." He wiped his nose and shook his head. "Only one way to go. Through that...that portal. And we were in a land of snow and ice. Lost. Ice sculptures and posters everywhere."

"Posters of who?" I asked.

Brian pointed at Dylan.

A curt woman's voice called from the doorway. "What are you doing in here?"

I wheeled around to see a frumpy nurse standing in the doorway. She had a large, oval face with dark eyebrows almost connected together and drawn down in a frown.

She stomped forward. "Get out!"

"B-but we're visiting," Jade said.

She swatted at Thomas, who was standing closest, He flinched and ran out, and we all followed behind him.

The nurse called from the room. "Go now. Get your bums out of here. Visiting's been over an hour ago. I let his mum stay, but he needs to rest. What are your names? You on the registry?"

We hurried down the hall to the elevator, and Jade asked, "Why did the woman downstairs say we had time?"

I shook my head. "Don't know."

We reached the elevator, and it dinged, the doors opening. The scent of peach perfume wafted to us, and then the elderly woman from Tales front desk stepped out, using a cane. She stopped in front of us.

I huddled close to Dylan. She raised her glasses on her nose, scanned each of us, and stopped on Dylan.

"Oh, there you are. I think you had better come with me."

She pointed to a nearby room that said Administration on the door. "Your family has been looking for you. You should come call them."

"M-my family?" Dylan stammered.

She smiled, and a chill tingled over my body.

I grabbed Dylan's hand and pulled him. He looked up to me, and I shook my head.

Dylan spoke in a low voice. "I can't now."

Her head cocked to one side, and a frown formed. "Why is that? You don't want to talk to your family?"

Dylan stared down at the coin in his hand and backed up, saying, "Because... because..." His voice raised several notches. "Because there's a fire alarm."

The old woman's mouth turned down and anger frothed underneath. She stepped forward, shoved Thomas out of the way, and reached for Dylan's arm. "Listen here, lad—"

Thomas stumbled into the wall, and his elbow pressed down on the fire alarm switch. A siren blurted out close to us, and the elder woman cringed and covered her ears.

I yanked on Dylan, grabbed Jade's hand, and called over my shoulder, "Come on, Thomas!"

I sprinted to the door that said Emergency Exit, stopped at the doorway, and let everyone through.

I looked up. The old woman stared at us, grimacing in pain, and continued to hold her hands over her ears. The second bank of elevators opened, and three white wolves stepped out to huddle around her. I swallowed, turned, and flew down the stairs.

Jade and Dylan were a flight down, waiting for me, and I flapped my hands at them. "Run! Run! Wolves!"

Two police officers were in the lobby and held their hands out to stop us.

I pointed to the exit door. "Fourth floor! A bloody mess!" They ran around us and up the stairs.

Dylan hurried ahead of me but slid to a stop at the front window. The snow had accumulated, and there was a thick layer on the sidewalk and street.

"Oh, bloody heck, look at that," Jade muttered. She glanced behind us. "Better out there than here with the creepy old lady. Let's go!"

Chapter Thirteen

WE RAN OUTSIDE into the snow, away from the hospital and across the street. A cold wind whipped at my face. We crossed the street and ran into a café. Several people were inside, on their phones, talking about the bizarre weather.

I caught my breath, my heart hammering in my chest.

Thomas pulled a stocking cap over his head. "You say you saw wolves?"

I told them what I had seen.

"W-who was she?" Jade asked.

I shrugged and turned to Dylan. "That was quite a coincidence, you saying that and then Thomas hitting the fire alarm. Lucky they're the old-fashioned kind, without the glass you have to break."

Dylan held the gold coin up. "Well, I think this did it. I did say my aunt was a witch. So Brian said a bearer just needs to speak his desire?"

Jade plucked it from Dylan's hand, and said, "He called it a charm. I think we ought to have a ride to 44 Lowre Few Lane before old creep woman comes back."

Dylan furrowed his brow and chuckled. "Nice thought." He snatched it back, flipped the coin in the air, and put it in his pocket. "Well, I second that."

Thomas pointed out the window. "It's that old woman!"

I stared out the window, and a knot formed in my throat. The old woman stood across the street, staring at us. Snow swirled around her.

A woman wearing a swaddle of clothing blocked my view and pulled open the door to the café. Snow blew in, and coldness whipped over me. I stared up at the woman's face.

"Ms. Griffin?"

Ms. Griffin smacked her coat with her hand, and snow fell off. I looked back out the window, but the creepy old woman was gone.

Ms. Griffin removed her hood scarf and looked down at us, putting her hands on her hips. "I was just leaving the nursing home after seeing me mum. Thought about getting hot tea in the bitter cold when I see four kids running from the hospital across the street. One red hair. And one Asian." She shook her head. "What are you all doing here?"

Jade spoke first. "We went to visit Brian Kennedy."

Ms. Griffin placed her hands on her hips in a very concerned-teacher way. "You see the weather out there?" She waved her hand and said, "Come on then. Let me take you home. Town mayor is going to pass a curfew and order everyone into their homes."

The decision of what to do was not hard. She was an adult. We were kids. We followed her to her car and got inside. I sat in the back with Dylan and Thomas, and Jade was in the front.

Ms. Griffin turned on the car and peered out the window. "Never seen anything like this." She shivered and rotated the dial to turn up the heater. "Colton, they staying at your house?" she asked over her shoulder.

"Yes, ma'am," I answered.

"How did you get out here to the hospital?" Ms. Griffin glanced in the rearview.

"The bus," Jade and I answered at the same time.

"Oh, my," Ms. Griffin said, rubbing her hands in front of the vent. "Good thing I came when I did. Mr. O'Leary, how did you get with these characters? I thought your uncle picked you up."

Thomas shrugged.

I elbowed him and whispered, "She can't hear a shrug." Then I leaned up. "His uncle had a family emergency. Dropped him off."

Ms. Griffin shook her head. "Oh, dear. So many unpleasantries today. And then this news about Erin going missing. Just horrible. You children really should not be venturing out."

I sat on my hands and secretly felt relieved we were not going to Ronan's house. But guilt tugged at me. Erin was over there.

I glanced to Dylan, then to Ms. Griffin driving. Jade was looking back at me, her eyes helpless.

Dylan whispered to me, "We're going to get farther away."

"What should I say?" I asked. "You have your aunt's coin. How's it work?"

Dylan wrung his hands and stared out the window. He brought the coin from his pocket, stared at it, and blurted out, "Uh, Ms. Griffin. Can you take me to my house?"

Ms. Griffin looked up into the rearview mirror and smiled. "Of course. Your aunt home?"

Dylan nodded. "She was at a friend's earlier, but she's now home. She lives really close."

"Where you live?"

"Fifty Lowre Few Lane. Take a left up at the next light."

I stared at Dylan and mouthed, "What are we going to do?"

Dylan was biting his lip, and he shook his head. My heart beat fast, and my palms grew sweaty. I didn't want Dylan to leave us, and I knew he would try to find his aunt on his own. I felt choked and caught Jade looking back at me. The same thought must have been going through her mind.

I had an idea. I put my hand over the coin in Dylan's hand and took it.

I licked my lips. "Ms. Griffin?"

She was leaned over the steering wheel. The windshield wipers were working hard whipping the snow off the window. She glanced up to the rearview mirror and back down.

"D-don't you live outside of town?" I asked. "I don't want you to get stuck in the snow. I think we should all stay at Dylan's, and you get on your way."

Ms. Griffin stared out through the front windshield, and I wasn't sure if she'd heard me.

Jade glanced back at me and to Ms. Griffin, then repeated the pattern. Jade finally leaned up and said in a timid voice, "Ms. Griffin?"

"Your parents will be worried sick about you. I should—"

Dylan interrupted. "It's okay. They were coming over anyway because of the storm."

Jade chirped up. "Besides, we were going to Dylan's house to, uh, to practice—"

Thomas stuck a finger in the air. "To practice for choir!"

Jade's mouth fell open, and she whipped her gaze back toward Thomas. If looks could kill...

Ms. Griffin glanced in the rearview mirror, and I felt tiny. It was over. Of all the things to say. Thomas's voice was a cross between a frog and a broken whistle; he was not choir material. Not to mention, he played hockey. Neither I nor Dylan was in any choir. And for that matter, Ms. Griffin was in the town's choir. Irish folk music was her love. The cherry on top was that she was friends with the school's teacher who held choir class.

To say Ms. Griffin's response shocked me would be an understatement. "Oh, how wonderful! That makes sense. I have been in the choir since I was a wee girl, you know that?" She looked up in the rearview mirror. I felt my head nodding. Thomas was nodding, too, a stupid grin on his face.

"You practicing for the Christmas play?" she asked.

"Yes, ma'am." Jade was actually in the choir. "'While Shepherds Watched Their Flocks' has been tough."

Ms. Griffin shivered and smiled. "Well, good luck to you children."

Dylan snatched the coin from me. "Can you let us out here? It's just a block away. Our streets have been shut down for the last week. Some, uh, some broken sewer line. You'll regret it if you go."

"Oh, dear. That's horrible. And with all this freezing, I'm certain that has made a mess."

"You have no idea," Dylan replied.

She slowed the car and put it in park. "How far is it?"

"It's just there. Can you see it?" Dylan pointed between the seats to a house on the corner. "See?"

The snow was heavy, and we were half a block from Lowre Few Lane on a street I could not remember. But in order to get to Dylan's house, we needed to take a left at the corner, go two blocks, past 44 Lowre Few Lane, and then back up a hill. It could not logically be anywhere in sight. Not to mention there was no construction in front of us for a supposed broken sewer pipe. Dylan had gotten too cocky and made a huge blunder. Now it was all over.

Another thunderbolt.

"Oh, that's not far at all. Well, be careful, children," Ms. Griffin answered.

I opened my door and got out. Thomas, Dylan, and Jade were behind me. On the sidewalk, I leaned through the car's open door and said my farewell. "Thank you, ma'am."

"You're welcome, Mr. Ryan. Keep bundled up and get out of this storm. Oh, be careful of the ice spiders. And remember, they don't like to skate," Ms. Griffin said.

I balked and said, "*What?*"

She looked at me and offered me a sweet smile. "What's that, Mr. Ryan?"

"What'd you just say?"

"I said be careful of the ice, dear."

I nodded. "O-okay."

Ms. Griffin touched her head, and I heard her mutter, "I'm going to need to take meself a nice bubbly bath. It's been a long day."

I shut the door, and Ms. Griffin turned her car around and pulled away.

"What in the blimey heck just happened?" Jade said. "I've never seen Ms. Griffin so thick-skulled."

Thomas mused. "Could be she took a stop at the pub earlier. Me uncle does it all the time. His trolley is never quite on the track afterward."

I cocked my thumb to Dylan, who had the gold coin in his palm. "The bearer just needs to speak his desire. If you're holding the coin, I think you just need to say what you want. I know it sounds crazy, but..." I shrugged.

Jade stared down at the coin. "Your aunt did that?" She looked up to Dylan.

Dylan grinned. "Well, I did say she was a witch." Dylan turned and put it back in his pocket. "Well, guys, let's count on our good luck. Come on. It's not far." He started away.

I trotted to him, and Thomas and Jade came up to my side. I stared into the sky where the snow fell in sheets. I thought about the bus driver's joke. He indeed might need to get a sleigh of dogs; this was turning into a blizzard.

I told everyone what Ms. Griffin had said about how ice spiders couldn't skate.

Thomas shook his head. "I don't like bloody spiders."

"What do you think that meant?" Jade asked.

"Probably find out sooner than later," Dylan said in front of us.

We reached the corner on Lowre Few Lane and stared across the intersection. There was an ambulance, and the medics had someone on a gurney. There were IVs attached to the person, who was under a swaddle of blankets.

I looked around. "There are no cars."

I stepped across the street and peered closer. The medics were speaking on their walkie-talkies. I stopped midstep, and Dylan bumped into me.

"What?" he asked.

"I-I think it's David. Brian's brother."

Dylan whipped his head around and stared at the person on the gurney. They were about to load him into the ambulance. Dylan sprinted toward the vehicle.

Jade and Thomas came closer. "What is it?" Jade asked.

I licked my cracked lips. "Brian's brother. David. He's back."

Jade's jaw dropped open. "What?"

"What's Dylan doing?" Thomas asked.

I shrugged. The medics had looked down at the sudden appearance of Dylan, seeming to be taken off guard that anyone would be out in the snow. David lifted his head and was speaking to Dylan.

The medic pushed Dylan back. "Scram, lad. Get home before you freeze." Dylan made to argue, and the medic pointed. "I'm calling the coppers, lad."

Dylan turned and jogged back to us. His face was pale.

I leaned up. "Was it David?"

Dylan nodded but didn't say anything.

"What did David say?" Jade asked.

Dylan wiped his mouth and stared at Jade with blank eyes.

"Dylan," I said.

Dylan looked at me. "H-he said a woman freed him. He said she went to save a little girl."

"Your aunt saved him," I said.

Dylan nodded. "Had to be."

Chapter Fourteen

NONE OF US spoke as we walked down Lowre Few Lane. Each of us had our head down, and we braced ourselves against the snow whipping into us.

My feet sank into a layer of snow that now covered the old cobble street and sidewalk. Ice pelted and stung my face. I cinched the front of my coat with both hands, trying to make it warmer.

Dylan still looked distant after seeing David. He was the only one of us four who didn't appear to be cold. He wore a jacket. I had earlier offered him a couple of heavy wool jackets that had been my father's when he was a boy, and I'd said he wouldn't mind if he knew it was helping a kid keep warm. Dylan had shaken his head and taken the jacket I wore in between the melting frost and spring. I thought he'd placed a stocking cap and gloves in his bag, but he now wore none. His hair was covered with white flakes.

He glanced toward me and forced a smile. "Not exactly how I saw this night going."

I nodded. "Aren't you cold?" I pointed down at his hands. "I have some extra mittens. You want them? You might get frostbite."

He looked down at his hands, made fists, and turned to me. He offered me a cockeyed grin, the lovely dimples forming on one side. "They're actually warm. I don't even notice it. See?" He placed the palm of his hand on my cheek. Heat radiated from his skin, and then pulled his hand back. "It's like that every winter. Weird, huh?"

I never wanted to wash my cheek again. I merely nodded.

"Dylan," Jade said, "you want to check your aunt's house again? See if she came back?"

Dylan wiped the wetness from his face and pushed his bangs back. "Um, I guess so. Let's try that first."

We needed to climb this hill, go down the next, pass Ronan's house, go back up the incline, and there'd be Dylan's home.

We came near the top of the hill. The street was slicker, and I suggested we walk in the weedy yards. I stepped toward the side, where there were several trees, and the frozen grass crunched under my feet. I stepped close to a small shack and had a perfect view to the bottom of the hill. Visibility was not great, but there was Ronan's house. The snow was falling even heavier in this area. In fact, it was even colder here than it had been a hundred feet back. Everyone came up behind me and stared down.

I wiped my runny nose. "You think it'll be hard to get into Ronan's world if we have to go?"

"Brian said he and his brother got inside. It didn't sound hard," Dylan answered.

Jade brought out her phone. "I'm going to call Erin again." She stared at the screen, pushing buttons on the side. "It's not even working now. Colton, let me see yours?"

I brought mine out. "Wait." I tried to turn it on, but it didn't start. "Blimey thing is dead." I looked up. "You think Ronan's world did something?"

Jade shrugged and stared down at her phone before putting it inside her pocket. "Maybe. But how did Erin call us?"

That was a good question.

"I think Ronan's powers are growing in this world. You saw the weather report. It said the snow was starting from somewhere inside Arklow. Duh. From here. And it's even colder here than it was a block away." Dylan put his hands up. "I'm just saying." He made a nervous laugh. "And I have this instinct."

"What?" I asked.

"I think Ronan is luring me into his world," Dylan said.

"Lads." Jade shook her head. "I have a bad feeling. I think we shouldn't do this."

Dylan turned to her. It was obvious he was set on going into Ronan's house to find his aunt. I would not let him go alone. We either had to go with him or convince him this was a foolish errand.

Jade put her hands up to Dylan. "Oy, wait, Dylan. We can just stay at your aunt's house. Talk things over. I mean, what are we going to do when we get there? Or if we come across this Ronan? W-we're just twelve-year-olds."

Dylan straightened and crossed his arms. "I turned thirteen October first."

"I'm going to be thirteen next month," I said and pointed to Thomas who was looking in the opposite direction. "And oaf here is almost fourteen." I turned toward Thomas and my voice rose. "Oy, Thomas, what are you ogling at? You like to join the conversation?"

Thomas's jaw worked, and when he turned to me, his eyes were large and spooked. "W-wolves." Thomas pointed behind me, and I snapped my attention in the direction of his finger.

"Pete's sake!" I stepped back and fell hard on my butt.

There were white wolves behind us, too many to count. They were on both sides of the street and on some lawns and porches of the nearby homes. As one pack, they slunk forward, heading toward us. I scrambled up to my feet, remembered their speed, and spun around, searching for shelter. There was the shack beside us with a lock on its handle.

"Colton," Thomas said.

I paid him no attention, though, and scanned the area. Dylan wiggled his hand into his pocket to pull out his gold coin, but it fumbled from his fingers. The nearest house was a hundred feet away.

I pointed. "That house!"

"Colton!" Thomas repeated.

I turned to him. "What!"

Thomas picked up the coin, his eyes bright. "We just need a sled!"

I shook my head, having no words for that absurdity. I turned to Jade and Dylan. "Run!"

Jade was staring at the pack and stepped backward, her hip bumping into the shack door. The lock fell off the front latch and plopped down into the snow. The owner must have never locked it. The door flew open, and several items burst out from inside. Something slid in front of Thomas's feet.

A long sleigh.

Thomas gave out a short high-pitched laugh. He handed the coin back and hauled the sled out to the middle of the road.

Thomas knelt down on it with his knees. He waved for us to join him. Dylan got on behind Thomas, and Jade came next. I was last and wrapped my arms around Jade. Thomas leaned out and pushed on the ground to either side with his gangly arms. We barely moved at first, and then gathered speed.

Thomas settled back down and cheered, "Brilliant!"

A crisp wind blew over my face. We sped down the hill fast. I dared not move and kept the side of my face pressed up against Jade's back. Trees and the few houses that were along the street blurred by.

We were in the air for a moment, and Thomas yelled out, "Woo-hoo!"

When the sleigh landed, I jarred forward and rocked sideways, about to fall off. I would have probably taken everyone. Dylan leaned the opposite direction and pulled everyone upright. The sleigh turned and pointed at an angle toward the curb. We hit the edge, flew up in the air, and landed in a snowfield with tall, frozen weeds that snapped one after the other, their stalks slapping into my face. A thick oak approached fast, but the sleigh was losing its momentum. It came to an abrupt stop, its nose barely a hand-width away from the trunk.

I was up on my feet and looking the way we'd just come. Dylan and Jade got up next.

"I don't see them," I said.

I spoke too soon. Several wolves came up over the crest and made a dash toward us.

Ronan's house was on the other side, and it would not be a far run.

"They're coming from the other direction too!" Dylan said behind me.

I turned around, and indeed, there were wolves close to Dylan's home and advancing toward us fast. We were trapped in the middle.

Dylan didn't hesitate but grabbed Jade's hand and darted toward Ronan's house, yelling over his shoulder, "Colton, come on. We have no choice now."

I yanked on Thomas's arm. He sat in a pile of snow by the sleigh, a large grin on his face. He was still lost to the thrill of the downhill ride we had just taken.

"Thomas!" I said.

He startled and looked up to me.

"Get your bum moving," I yelled.

Thomas looked both ways and no doubt saw the approaching pack. He was up on his feet a second later and darted toward Ronan's house. He had longer legs, and he gained a lead over me. He looked over his shoulder and waved for me to hurry.

Jade and Dylan made their way down the winding driveway toward the front porch. The wolf statues were gone, and the door was cracked open. Dylan halted at the base of the porch, his hand on the rail, and gawked up at the door. Jade bumped into his back. Thomas came behind them, and I made it finally, then stooped over, catching my breath.

I glanced behind me. The ground was moving, and I realized I was seeing white wolves coming down the street. "*Go, guys!*" I yelled.

Dylan and Jade jumped at my voice and flew up the stairs. I followed Thomas through the door and stood in a living room that had dirty furniture with torn fabric. The walls were cracked everywhere, and in a few places were gaping holes. I slammed the door behind me, locking the two bolts. A dreary hallway was on our left, and another room in front had to be the kitchen.

Thomas, Jade, and Dylan shoved a hutch up against the door.

"*Oh, mannn,*" Dylan muttered, a tone of terror underscoring his voice. "I know why that old woman's smell was familiar."

"W-what?" Peach perfume filled my nostrils, and I cringed.

"What are you talking about?" Jade squeaked.

Dylan spoke, his voice a whisper. "She smelled like this house."

The boards squeaked in the kitchen. A hunched-over shadow danced over the walls, and an elderly woman with large glasses and white hair hobbled out holding a cane. Wolf earrings dangled from each ear. It was the old woman from the hospital. She smirked, and Thomas grabbed my shoulder.

"C-Colton. Her teeth."

I backed up into Thomas. Her teeth did look a bit too long in her mouth. She pushed up her glasses, and she changed in front of our eyes.

Jade let out a scream.

A humongous, cloaked figure stood in front of us, the face covered by a hood. A low baritone boomed out. "Took you all long enough." Had to be Ronan. "You got away from me at the hospital. That witch must have given you a charm. But there's nowhere to hide now."

The wall and furniture behind him vanished, and in its place was a translucent watery substance that rippled. In the distance was the silhouette of a vast-sized castle.

I was staring at the magical portal that Erin must have been looking through earlier.

Two wolves made of stone stepped out of the portal next to Ronan. They were the wolf statues that had been by the porch base.

Dylan backed up and whispered, "R-run."

Ronan transformed before our eyes once again, but this time into something beyond human. The cloak ripped from the body, and hair grew at a rapid rate over him.

I spotted the coin in Dylan's hand. It was glowing. I grabbed it and shouted, "Give us silver."

A door creaked under the stairwell, and I stepped up and grabbed the doorknob. Ronan was now a terrifying werewolf with razor-sharp teeth, clawed hands, and emblazoned blue eyes.

I yanked on the doorknob, and plates, knives, forks, spoons, and all sorts of dinnerware made of silver spilled out onto the floor. I dropped the coin and stared down in horror, trying to see where it went. I glanced up. Ronan raised an arm defensively, howled in pain, and hunkered down.

Dylan crumpled to his knees, his chin hung down to his chest. I grabbed under his arm, and yelled, "Thomas, grab him!"

Thomas grabbed under his other arm and lifted Dylan up.

Jade pointed. "Look!" The coin had risen in the air. It shone a luminescent gold, and it moved up the stairs. "Follow it."

Thomas and I towed Dylan up the stairs. Dylan helped to a small degree, shuffling his feet up on each step. At the top of the stairs, Thomas and I paused to catch our breaths and let Dylan down.

Dylan touched his head and said, "That was too much silver."

A ruckus of *clinks* and *chinks* came from down below, and a sea of silverware spilled out at the base of the stairs. Two stone wolves stared up at us from the bottom, their eyes a fierce red.

"Hey, it's moving," Jade said. The gold orb zipped down the hall and into a room at the end.

I grabbed Dylan's arm, but he was up on his feet. "Got it now." He rushed ahead of us, and I followed him into a master-sized bedroom. It had scattered worn furniture covered in cobwebs and dust. I slammed the door behind us and threw the bolt. A few moments later, the door rattled, and I cringed and backed away from it.

Thomas stared at the door. "Colton, there's something trying to get in."

"I know, Thomas," I said.

"What's it doing now?" Dylan asked and pointed up at the orb. It rose in the air, and without warning, four fiery gold marbles split from it and moved in a blur. One flew to me, and I touched my chest where it had entered. I felt nothing, though. I looked up, to find everyone else was touching their chests too.

The doorframe rattled hard, and I flinched.

Dylan spoke from across the room. "Look, guys."

The far wall was no longer solid but an archway. On the other side was a field of green grass. Completely surreal.

Dylan hesitated at the wall and touched it. His fingertips appeared to dip into water. The scene in front of us rippled, and Dylan turned around and smiled.

"Cool." He beckoned us. "What are we waiting for? Let's go." He stepped forward, and then he was on the other side, standing in the field. Jade followed him, and then Thomas.

I took one step inside. Behind me, wood splintering and the door broke open. The temperature rose several degrees at once. A fresh scent filled the air, and the top of stalks of grass brushed my hand.

I pushed Thomas. "Go, guys. Run..."

I looked behind me, surprised I wasn't staring inside a room, but at a field of waist-high grass that went as far as my eyes could see. On one side of me, a river wound through the field with trees dotted around it, their bark purple and leaves blue. They sparkled in the sun. We were up high on some sort of peak, and a vast lake lay beneath us and beyond that were mountains.

Aunt Ruth's voice spoke behind me. "I'm glad you made it to Weredom."

Chapter Fifteen

I WHIRLED AROUND toward the direction of Aunt Ruth's voice. Hovering a few feet over the stalk heads was a radiant light, and I realized I was staring at Aunt Ruth. *Sort of.* She was a hologram projected in front of us, wearing an overcoat, gloves, and a stocking hat.

Dylan came up beside me and bleated, "Aunt Ruth!" He turned to us, his eyes large, and then looked back to her. His tongue appeared to be in knots, and he stammered, "W-what—"

Aunt Ruth held up her mittened hands. "Quiet, lad. We have little time." She leaned forward. "I see Brian gave you the charm. It protects you against Ronan's curses. He can't turn you into icicles, which you should be grateful for. But it's also a key that got you here rather than just outside the keep of Ronan's castle."

Thomas scratched his head. "Charm?"

Aunt Ruth furrowed her brow. "The gold coin, lad. Who are you?"

"Oh, me?" Thomas asked, and smiled. "Thomas O'Leary."

"Thomas O'Leary. Very well. Well done with the sleigh earlier. But let's keep our tongues in our mouths, shall we? Time is short. The more I talk, the more likely Ronan can find me. I gather you know Ronan is not only a werewolf but also a sorcerer?"

I caught everyone's eyes, and we all nodded.

"Good. Ronan came from this world long ago. It's where the werewolves hail from. It's called Weredom. Ronan has limited powers in your world. He can shapeshift, though, and order his wolves to do his bidding. His powers are growing strong at his old house because of the snow. The more it freezes, the more powerful he is there. But in here...his abilities are vast." Aunt Ruth flinched, looked behind her, and talked to someone.

"Can't Ronan find us here?" Jade whispered to me.

I threw my hands up in the air. I had no idea.

Aunt Ruth turned back around and whispered in an urgent matter. "Ronan is coming. Come to Ronan's Castle, to the black tower. That's where we'll be. He doesn't know where you're at, so you're a step ahead."

Someone came up to Aunt Ruth's side. Erin.

Aunt Ruth continued quietly. "The charms are now inside each of you. You each have two charms to make realized. All you need to do is say *Realize*, then say whatever you want. But this part is important—"

A low, steady growl startled Aunt Ruth. She whirled around to look behind her.

"*Run!*" Aunt Ruth harshly whispered.

Aunt Ruth and Erin were gone. An opening appeared far in the background, and Ronan's hooded silhouette stepped inside the doorway. The two stone wolves with their ruby red eyes flanked him on either side.

Ronan pushed his hood back and revealed a bushy head and beard. He strode forward until his midsection was in view. He reached toward us, and I took a step back. I expected his hand to come through, only this was not a doorway but something akin to a teleconference device. Except that this was magic.

Ronan hunched down so we could all see his wiry and shaggy bearded face. Ronan's eyes were wild, and he smirked at us, one of his hands fiddling with his grisly beard.

"Ah, she put you *there*. Clever." He pointed to Dylan and said, "Give him to me, and I'll leave your world alone. You do understand my powers are growing in your world now. See."

He snapped his fingers.

The image changed, and I was staring at the inside of my home. My breath caught. It was surrounded by white wolves. The view changed to show Georgia on the couch. She was snoring one second, and in the next, she turned to ice before my eyes.

The finger snap happened again.

Ms. Griffin was in her bubble bath, scooted all the way down. Her face was the only thing visible. She, too, turned to ice.

Fingers snapped.

Jade let out a sharp cry. Cousin Jane was frozen.

Thomas whimpered. His uncle was frozen.

Ronan's scraggly bearded face returned. "Give him to me. I'll let your family go. Leave you in peace."

"Y-you can't have him!" Jade screamed.

The image showed Ronan again. He sneered, "Very well." The radiating light was gone. In front of us was only a vast field of green grass with scattered purplish trees.

"U-uh," I stammered and shook my head in disbelief. "He turned them into ice." I licked my lips. "What happens when my dad returns? H-he'll..." I couldn't bear the thought.

Dylan touched my arm. "Colton."

I looked to him.

"We need to get to my aunt. She can return everything back to normal."

I nodded. "R-right."

"Let's go," Jade said.

"Which way?" Thomas asked.

Dylan pointed over my shoulder. A roaring waterfall plummeted off a ledge in the distance. Beyond a picturesque land filled with dark blue-leafed trees was a great lake and, in the far distance, a mountain range with snowy peaks. On one peak the silhouette of a vast castle stretched high into the air.

"Right," I said. "I guess that makes it easy."

Thomas cracked. "Bloody sake, we'll make it there by next Hollow's Eve."

"Aunt Ruth said we each get, uh, two charms to make realized? That mean what I think?" I asked.

Jade pointed up. "Right, so she calls them charms. In our world, they made coincidences happen. Dylan said there was a fire alarm, and Thomas just happened to run into a fire alarm. I said I wanted a ride from the hospital to 44 Lowre Few Road, and it coincidentally happened. We said we wanted to be dropped off a block from his home, and Ms. Griffin let us out in a snowstorm. And I think it was getting stronger closer to the house. Then Thomas thought of the sleigh, and it fell out of that ol' shack. So coincidences there; and here it's probably more powerful."

Thomas looked between us and tapped his chin. "She said to use a word, though. What was it...?"

I forgot too.

"Oh, boy. Guys, uh, we need to go. *Like now*," Dylan said from behind me.

I turned to him, and he pushed on my chest and then shoved Jade.

"Oy, what is it?" I asked, looking over Dylan's head.

The reason was quite clear. The sky had gone from sunny to a dark, brooding gray. In the distance, several gigantic tornado funnels had formed, and they were destroying everything in their paths. They spewed up green stalks of grass and shredded the purple trees. The huge funnels moved at a swift pace across the field toward us.

I turned and sprinted forward through the sea of grass. Jade and Dylan were at my side, and Thomas took the lead. Adrenaline pumped through my body as a series of sharp snaps told us the field was being torn up.

The river was now at our side, the ground becoming soggier and harder to move on. I half turned. Two funnels, each about the size of a house, were beelining toward us. The river crossed in front of us, and we were trapped. Everyone slowed, their eyes huge, and looked back at the inevitable.

My feet were sticking, and then the word came to me. *Realize.*

I envisioned a path under my feet that crossed over the water. "Realize a footpath," I shouted.

In a blink of an eye, the tall, thick grass was gone, and a solid path made of grass bricks manifested itself under my feet, crossing over like a bridge and moving along the river.

"Look! You can make things with your mind!" I yelled.

I darted forward, over the bridge, with my friends at my back. Thomas flew past me once again and hefted up a small hill toward the crest. I looked back, and Jade was far in the rear, Dylan right behind me.

Dylan pointed ahead, yelling, *"Colton!"*

When I turned, Thomas had stopped; his arms flailed at his side as if he was trying to regain his balance. He was standing at the edge of a cliff. I bumped into Thomas's back and threw him off balance even more. My arms flew around his waist to keep him from falling, but it was too late. We were both tipping forward. Dylan grabbed my shoulder and pulled Thomas and me back.

Dylan came to my side and peeked over the edge. I stared too. A waterfall plunged down and disappeared into a fog, making a rainbow of sparkling colors. Down the cliff face ran a myriad of bright-colored green vines.

Thomas sighed in front of me, saying, "That was bloody cl—"

He never finished. Jade careened straight into Dylan's back. She had been gawking behind her at the towering funnels.

We all four tipped forward and plummeted down. Thomas covered his eyes with one hand. The air rushed past my ears, water misted me, and the fog approached fast.

Dylan shouted, "Realize Slippin' Slide Land!"

I barely registered it in my terrified state, but the vines from the rock face untangled and formed a tubular spiral that went downward. Dylan disappeared into the opening of the slide, and then Thomas, who shrieked out in delight inside the large vine-made pipe. The top of this freeform slide moved a few feet to the left so the gaping hole was right under me. I flew inside the orifice and whipped around in circles over and over, too many times to count, until nausea set in. Thomas's raucous hoots echoed back to me. Jade was far behind and shrieking in terror.

The slide changed from a corkscrew to a sheer drop. My back was off the surface, and I descended at an inconceivable pace, my stomach in my mouth, too petrified to scream. Finally, my back skimmed over a soft, slick surface again and the incline became a gentler slope, my speed decreasing. The angle plateaued, and then I was out of the enclosed slide. A sun beamed down on me as I slowed to a stop, out of breath.

Thomas and Dylan were standing to the side, Thomas clapping and hopping up and down like a complete fool.

Dylan grinned down at me and asked, "Fun, huh?"

"What the devil was that—"

Jade's screams reached me, and I looked over my shoulder. She popped out of the vine tunnel and came to a stop a few feet from me. She sat up straight, her eyes huge as saucers, her mouth agape. She covered her chest with one hand and took in gulps of breath.

I checked out the tube slide everyone had just come down. It extended far up the mountainside at a steep angle, formed in a spiral, which disappeared into the hazy fog where we had all fallen. The vines unraveled before my eyes and, once again, attached to the side of the mountain. The slide was gone.

"Look," Dylan said, pointing up into the air. Among the cloudy fog, the funnels that had almost devoured us swirled high over our heads. Trees and grass whirled around at high speeds. The tornadoes headed through more clouds and were soon past us. They looked to be carrying their haul toward the lake and probably Ronan's castle. No doubt he planned to capture us with his magical storm.

I pushed my fingers through my hair and looked around me. Several hundred feet away, the base of the waterfall poured into a large pool. Frothy water spewed up in the air. Around the pond, where the river began, were green leafy plants with huge oblong leaves. The river crawled past me and wound through slender trees that had peculiar blue-crystal leaves. My gaze followed the river up to a bend, and I assumed it kept going until it reached the lake I had seen earlier.

Jade got up and stammered, "H-how did that slide appear from nowhere?"

Dylan grinned. "In Portland, my parents take me to a water park called Slippin' and Slidin'. They have wicked cool slides." He pointed behind me. "But that was way cooler."

"Right," Jade said. "T-that's all brilliant and everything." She fixed her hair, which stuck out at odd angles. "But how did Portland bloody get here?"

"We just think of something in our mind, and it then becomes real. We just need to say *Realize* so the thought is realized," I answered.

Thomas jabbed a finger in the air. "Realize large cheesy from Green Irish Pizza!"

I stared at Thomas and looked around. Everyone else was doing the same. Crystals from a nearby tree blew up in the air, swirled in around, and came toward us. I cringed from the approaching dustbowl. It looked like a swarm of bees were about to attack us. The specks darted at Thomas's feet and hardened into a flat disk. I squatted down and stared at the sculpture the particles had formed. It was a mold of a cheesy pizza. I touched it, and it was moist and squishy. I tore at it, and a piece of blue leaf dangled between my fingers.

"Oy, you can't eat this."

Dylan tapped his chin. "Um, yeah. I think it has to be created by the materials around us. So, Colton thought of a sidewalk and the grass turned into a walkway. I thought of a slide and voila with the vines." He turned to Thomas. "Sorry, man. But there's nothing around to make your pizza."

Thomas frowned, and I did too. I was hungry and had only eaten just a bit of dinner. I muttered, "Wish there was a Supermac's store."

Thomas's eyes brightened and he opened his mouth. "Real—"

My hand flew up and covered his mouth. Muffled words spilled out from between my fingers.

"You just wasted one, you plonk. And we only get two. So whatever you were going to say, you might ask us first. I'm pretty certain they can't build Supermac's here either," I said.

I removed my hand. Thomas's mouth turned downward, his eyes saddened, a regular crestfallen look.

Jade gazed with intensity at the river, and I regarded it, too, asking, "What?"

Every few moments, a fish spiraled out from the surface, twirled in the air, and plopped back into the water.

A smirk formed on Jade's face. "I have the picture in me head. Realize cooked fish."

A hole appeared in the ground before me, and rocks assembled on the edge. A pile of kindling formed in the center, and three rows of spits were laid out over the top. Two flat rocks glided through the air from the nearby forest and scraped against one another at the base. Sparks spewed up, a fire was lit, and within a second, it was a roaring blaze. There was a splashing noise from the river, foaming water raised from the surface, and a dark shadow darted in our direction.

Within two more blinks of an eye, there were three rows of cook-blackened fish rotating over red embers.

Thomas clapped Jade on the back, and said, "That was off the hook!" He turned to everyone with a huge grin that stretched from ear to ear.

I stared at him, my eyes blinking. Jade had the same look, her lower jaw hung down.

Dylan's mouth was an *O*.

Thomas's smile faded. "Wrong timing?"

Dylan's shocked expression transformed, and a half-cocked smile appeared. He brought his fist up and nodded. "Perfect, dude."

Thomas made a fist and bumped Dylan's, and then he winked. "Off the hook, dude."

We roared with laughter at that. And it was nice for a change after being chased by white wolves into a portal and then off a cliff by tornadoes. Felt very nice.

Chapter Sixteen

WE HAD EATEN dinner, and our bellies were full. The sun was setting over the distant mountain range, and a deep raw coldness set in around us. The warmth from our campfire was one bit of solace. I was also thankful for my coat, but it was not enough. I shivered close to the embers and stuck in twigs from a pile of sticks next to the fire so that the flames thickened.

We all sat close. Jade cozied up beside me. Even Dylan appeared to be cold, and he sat on my other side, leaning into me. Thomas snuggled close to Jade, hugged his knees, and was hunched over. The noise of his teeth rattling was clear.

I tried to distract myself from the cold and thought of meeting Dylan the first time. I remembered being mesmerized by those eyelashes. I breathed out and saw my breath. The memories of Georgia and the others being frozen intruded on my thoughts.

Snow flurries twirled down from the sky.

"C-Colton," Jade said, squeezing closer to me.

"W-what?" I asked, my teeth chattering.

"T-the river. Look."

I turned to discover the new moon's light reflecting from the glossy ice on the surface.

"Is Ronan doing this?" I asked.

"He no doubt tried to use those tornadoes to get us to him. Now, he must come our way. And I get the feeling that wherever he wants to go, so does a blizzard," Dylan answered.

Thomas chattered. "W-we're going to have blimey hypothermia before the night is over."

My mind worked. I knew the word, and it made sense.

Jade asked the question in my head. "Thomas, how do you know about that?"

"M-me hockey coach talks about it all the time. Tells us to stay busy on the ice and keep our heart rates up," Thomas answered.

"He's right," Dylan responded.

"W-we're supposed to be active all night? We'll be plum tired in the morning."

"No," Dylan said. "It's getting too cold. I think the temperature is going to drop even more. Without the sun, we're in trouble. I have an idea. But I need to check something." He got up from the ground and started away.

I looked up, frightened. "Wait, Dylan. Where are you going?"

His voice called back from the darkness. "I'll be right back. Chill out, dude."

I cocked my head to the side and asked out loud, "Chill out? What in the blooming world does that mean?"

"Is it some kind of blimey American humor?" Jade murmured from my side.

"M-maybe," Thomas said, his teeth continuing to chatter. "It's like saying going to the loo."

"Don't be a dope, Thomas," I replied. "That doesn't even make any sense."

Snaps of footsteps approached, and Dylan squatted by the campfire, holding his hand out. "Look, guys."

Inside his palm were the blue leaves I had seen on the purple trees. I picked up a leaf. The material was silky and soft.

"It feels like a feather," I marveled out loud.

"Yup," Dylan said. "And the forest is filled with them."

Thomas and Jade plucked one from Dylan's palm, and they, too, were awed.

Dylan brought his other hand from behind his back. "And look at this."

He held out a huge leaf from the lush green plants I had seen at the waterfall base. It was two feet in length and a foot across. I took it from him. I slid my fingers over it and pulled, and was surprised. It did not have the soft, fragile touch that I expected, that could be easily turned to a pulp. Instead, it had a smooth, fibrous feel that was resistant to being ripped in two.

Jade took it from me and put it on her cheek. She gripped it on either side and pulled, but it did not tear. She looked up, a half smile on her face. "Are you thinking what I'm thinking?"

"Silk dress?" Thomas guessed.

I shook my head. "No, Thomas." I held the feather up in the air. "We can make some wondrous blankets and coats from these."

I looked to Thomas, Dylan, and Jade. I pictured the objects I wanted formed, said the word *Realize,* and spoke my mind's desire of wanting Eskimo gear.

Within moments, we had four thick, fluffy, filled sleeping bags and puffy hooded coats. The outer sleeping bag and coat material were made from fibrous bark, filled with the leaves from trees in the forest. I had envisioned an ice hut in my mind as well, but it had just started snowing. Instead, a small wooden and oval-shaped shelter was built close to the fire.

I got inside the hut, and everyone followed me. There was not much room, but after I wiggled into my bag, we all nestled close together. My head was close to the opening. Thomas was on one side, and Dylan on the other. Jade's bag was between our feet along the wall structure.

I yawned, pulled my sleeping bag over my head, and asked, "How are we going to get to the castle? We're running out of, uh, charms."

Jade spoke, her voice muffled from inside her sleeping bag. "Colton, I'm too tired to think that far ahead."

"Right. Because tomorrow morning is so far away," I observed dryly.

"Don't fight, guys. We just need to get inside the castle. Then my aunt will help us," Dylan said.

"Dylan, why do you think she's trapped inside?" I asked. "How come she can't get out?"

His voice broke. "I-I don't know."

I reached up and put my hand on his arm. "I'm sorry. I'm sure she's fine."

Dylan wiped the wetness from his face and nodded.

Thomas shoved my shoulder. "Colton."

I shifted my position. "What, Thomas?"

"Look. Outside."

I stared out the hole in our hut. "Oy," I muttered.

"What is it?" Jade asked.

It was a blizzard. A blanket of flurries whipped about. The campfire was now covered in a snowdrift, and the river was barely visible.

Dylan was staring outside, too, and mumbled something. I picked up the words *Holy Cow*.

"Colton," Jade said, now up on her elbows. "What is it?"

I licked my lips and said, "Snow."

Thomas chortled. "A blimey snow squall is what that is. That's what my coach would call it. He said he got in one of these in Ontario, Canada, when he played hockey there."

Jade crawled up between Thomas and me and stared outside. "Oh, sure, look at that, would you? We made good timing, didn't we?"

"I bet Ronan wanted to freeze us," Dylan said.

"But we'd be dead," I said.

"I'm pretty sure he can use his magic to unfreeze us if he wanted. He said he'd let Georgia and the others go if you gave me up," Dylan replied.

It was eerily quiet after that comment. The image of Georgia being frozen was vivid.

Dylan's voice was subdued. "I'm sorry, guys. This is all my fault. You shouldn't be here. It's my aunt. I should be going."

I rolled over and faced Dylan. "Don't be a complete muppet, Dylan. You're our friend."

"Me mum says family does not have to be related by blood. Sometimes, it's just what's in your heart that matters," Jade said from my feet.

I couldn't see Dylan's face, but his hand darted up to an eye. "Thank you."

Thomas got up on his elbow. "Besides, this beats the heck out of me listening to me uncle snore and poot in his sleep."

Laughter followed this.

I laid my head back on a cushy pillow. The earlier incident with Erin was in my mind, and a sense of dread shuddered through me.

"I-I wish I had never said those words to Erin." A teardrop streaked from my eye down my face. "It just happened."

Jade crawled up to my bed and patted my leg. "It's okay, Colton. We all make mistakes. And she was just trying to make you jealous. Did a good job, too, from what I saw."

Dylan was up on his elbow, his brow furrowed. "What are you talking about?"

I sat up and remembered Dylan had been playing rugby. My faced turned red.

"Erin kept on about how you both were thick as thieves. Sounded like wedding bells were about to be rung, and you'd both have a nice cottage up in the hills," Thomas blurted out.

Dylan's mouth was opened, and his head made perceptible shakes. "What?"

Jade sighed. "Erin has the oogly-boogly eyes for Colton. She was saying you invited her to Portland, and she invited you on a trip. She was trying to make Colton jealous, and it, uh, well it worked."

"Oh," Dylan said and glanced to me. A smirk was on his face. "You like me?"

It was my turn to give him a confused look. "Are you a complete tool? I'd think it'd be obvious." I looked down.

Thomas laughed. "So. Who do you have oogly-boogly eyes for, Dylan?"

Dylan's hand reached up and squeezed mine. "I'll never say. But he's very cute and real smart."

I grinned in gratitude and held his hand for a second. I had never held a boy's hand like this before. Unless it was a formal shake or being forced to arm wrestle so other boys could laugh at me, this never happened. I liked it.

I laid my head down and stared at Dylan. He took his hand away to pull up his covers, then winked at me and turned onto his back. "Good night, guys."

"Good night," I said.

"Sleep tight," Jade said.

Thomas pinched me and said, "And don't let the bed bugs bite."

"Ouch," I cried and socked Thomas's arm. "Keep your hands to yourself, you neddy!"

Thomas chuckled. Dylan pinched me from the other side, and I hopped in the air.

I brought my blanket off my head and stared at Dylan with my best scowl.

Dylan grinned. "Oopsies. Sorry, bro. Thought you were Ronan's evil slug."

"Oh," I said. "Did you?" I was out of my bag and poking under Dylan's ribs, and he gave out a high-pitched giggle and tried to scoot away from me.

"And you look like his evil rodent. Does the rodent like this?"

Dylan bucked on the ground and said between laughs, "Noooo!"

Thomas climbed from his sleeping bag and poked his finger into my rib. I hollered and put my elbows down to block him.

Dylan got out of his bag, and he and Thomas double-teamed it, poking my sides or tickling my feet. I shrieked and thrashed on the ground.

Jade was the voice of reason. "Lads!"

We all froze and looked over to her.

She smiled. "Please quit acting like complete dopes. Go to bed."

I looked over to Thomas and Dylan. They smiled, and we turned to Jade and attacked. The highest-pitched squawks erupted.

Several minutes later, after Dylan hit his head on the hut ceiling, we decided it was time to stop. I got back inside my sleeping bag and pulled the cover over my head. A howling wind blew outside, mesmerizing me, and I fell asleep.

I awoke with a start. I had been dreaming. A nightmare would be a better description. I had been walking down Lowre Few Lane in a blinding fog and had lost everyone. I called out to Dylan, then Jade, and then Thomas. But no one answered. A growl sounded at my back, and I turned, thinking it was Dylan. But it was a gigantic beast that towered over my head with snarly claws and long fangs. Its eyes glowed cherry red, and a growl escaped from its snout. But it had actually spoken, asking if I would like to live alone in an icy world. That's when I startled awake.

I pushed my blanket off my face and observed the two sleeping bags on either side of me with bulky bodies inside them. At my feet was Jade. I turned to the door, but I couldn't see anything. The opening was packed with snow.

"Oh, blimey sake," Thomas muttered in a hoarse voice.

Thomas was up on his elbows, his head sticking out of his bag, hair standing in different directions on his head. He turned to me. "We're snowed in?"

Dylan rustled in his bag and sat straight up. His locks had fallen in front of his eyes, and he put his nose in the air. "Do you guys smell that?"

Jade rolled at my feet and rose into a sitting position as well, hands over her head and mouth open in a yawn.

She put a hand over her mouth and managed in a groggy voice, "You wouldn't believe the dream I had." She chuckled and looked to me, her eyes wide. She swiveled her gaze to Thomas, then stopped at Dylan. "Why are you guys here?" She regarded her surroundings and shrugged. "It wasn't a dream, was it?"

"If you dreamed we had thousands of white wolves chasing us, met an old woman who was really a werewolf, saw wolf statues that lived, went through a magical portal, and were then chased by tornadoes, then it's all real. If you were in a land with lollipop streetlamps and candy-cane roads, then it was all a dream. We haven't run into that... yet," I offered.

Dylan repeated his question, his nose up in the air. "Do you all smell that? That's fantastic." He grabbed his coat, put it on, and started to claw at the snow in the opening.

"Dylan," I said. "Where are you going?"

He stopped and looked back at me. "You're joking, right? Someone's cooking breakfast out there."

He turned his attention back to the blockade and scooped snow behind him like he was a dog. I guess he was, in some sense. Pieces of ice hit my face and went inside my bag. I put my hand up, trying to keep the cold wetness from being spouted out over me. Thomas half turned, shielded his face with his hands.

Jade protested. "Dylan, stop. It's a trap."

Dylan stopped and knelt on both knees. He cocked his head to the side. "Umm, I don't think so. It's not Ronan. I'd smell him. Or that weird old lady, who's Ronan, too, and wears peach perfume." He started to dig again.

"Dylan," I said. "Wait."

Dylan didn't quit. Daylight shone through the hole.

I shouted, "*Dylan!*"

He stopped, crawled backward, squatted by me with a grin. "Chill out, dude." He pinched and jiggled my cheek. "Time to get up, me wee little scab, and eat some breakfast to put meat on them thin bones." He giggled and moved at a quick pace, crawling through the hole, and was gone.

I rubbed my cheek and muttered, "I wish I knew what 'chill out' meant." I was soon out of my bag, grabbed my coat, pulled on my shoes, and said over my shoulder, "Come on. Let's go."

I wriggled through the hole. Bright sunlight hit me in the eyes, and the scent of cooked bacon and eggs filled my nose.

My stomach growled.

Chapter Seventeen

I CRAWLED OVER the snow-covered ground and got up to my feet. The scent of the campfire was in my nose, and I glanced in its direction—but froze. Not far from our hut was a huge sleigh with several black-and-white wolves fastened to it. They were all sitting on their haunches. A few were licking themselves or their partners.

A couple of wolves were staring at me. Each had one eye that was crystal blue while the other was emerald green.

I whirled around, and the cliff base that was several feet away was a sight. The waterfall had frozen in its place, only droplets trickling down over it.

I turned at Dylan's voice.

A small person with a white furry coat and hood sat on a stool close to a campfire, holding a frying pan full of sizzling eggs over the blaze. Copper plates were stacked close to the person's foot, and a large iron plate was close to the flames to keep the already-cooked fried eggs and bacon warm.

Dylan stood a few feet away from the stranger, talking. He appeared to be a bit timid but kept taking quick glances at the food.

I stepped cautiously up to the hooded person. The voice coming from under the hood seemed to be a girl's and had a lazy cadence. "Ne'er seen the lake frozen over in ages. I ne'er seen any small'ns like ya either for that matter. Quite irregular. Always a big'n that comes through that magic portal."

"Small'ns and big'ns?" Dylan said, brushing a hand through his hair.

"Yer accent is peculiar, laddy. I ne'er heard of it. Where ya from?"

"Oregon," Dylan said. "But my friends are from Ireland."

"Irye-land I heard of. Most Others are from that strange place. All of them with an accent I barely understand. But Or-ree-ghan? Tell me about your world."

Dylan laughed. "It's not a world. A state in the United States."

"Hmm, and what do they call ya in Or-ree-ghan?"

"Dylan."

Thomas spoke from behind me. "Willywigs and Irish turds. What is this?"

I glanced over my shoulder. Thomas and Jade stood next to the hut.

The girl flinched and half turned, but the hood blocked her face. She stood up from the stool, as tall as me with a rotund figure. She pushed the hood from her face and revealed a brown-skinned girl with long black hair who seemed about my age or a bit older. The hair had been braided on top of her head and came down in several plaits, a few of them draped around the front of her shoulder. Her cheekbones were square along with a rectangular jaw and thick eyebrows that rose up in something like pleased surprise.

She smiled, showed white teeth, and said, "Well, there's a sight for sore eyes. Two laddies and one lassy just rising from a deep slumber. I'm Meg of the Northerners."

She held her hands up in the air, thick mittens held by cords dangled from her sleeves, and waved for us to join. "Come on over, small'ns. Breakfast we shall eat. I understand yar off on to a dangerous journey to Ronan's castle. Can't say I recommend yar adventure, but then Witch Ruth of Iyre-Land made it quite clear I see ya there, and who am I to question her?"

Dylan squeaked out in shock, "*You know Aunt Ruth?*"

Meg waved her hand in dismissal. "O'course, Dylan of Or-ree-ghan. All Northerners know Witch Ruth of Iyre-Land. Tell me one who doesn't, and I show ya a pink dragon."

She cackled in laughter and sat back down on her stool. I couldn't help but wonder if there were dragons of any colors in this strange world.

She fixed a copper plate near her foot with eggs and bacon, and gave it to Dylan along with a rugged-looking fork. "Now small'ns," Meg said, "Let me find out yar names, and let's eat our hearty breakfast before it's a popsicle like the waterfall over yonder." She fixed each of us a plate, and I woofed mine down and had second helpings.

Jade finished her meal, wiped her mouth, and asked, "How did you know we were here?"

Meg started to put away the cooking gear and turned to Jade. "That was the easy part, Jade of Irye-Land."

"You can just call me Jade," Jade said and shrugged. "Might be easier."

Meg offered a soft smile. "Jade it is then, small'n."

"You can do that for all of us," I said.

Meg nodded. "Quite right, then."

She pulled something from inside a satchel at her side and held it out. A gold coin lay in her palm, and it rose up in the air and became a glowing source of light. Within a blink of an eye, it turned into a holographic map and showed the nearby river, the cliff behind us with the frozen waterfall, and four green specks near a hut. The four green dots were clearly us. It was a GPS system, but it was safe to assume this GPS was guided by magic rather than a satellite.

Meg's fist closed over the coin, and the hologram vanished. She put it back inside her satchel. "Lucky for ya and for me, Ronan froze the lake over last night." She bent over and started packing her stuff again. "Otherwise, I'd have to ferry over. That'd not do either. My dogs don't dare swim." She tittered at her own joke.

"You said Northerners? Is that your, uh, country?" I asked.

"Aye, it 'tis. Your name?"

"Colton."

"You're so young," Jade commented.

"Me?" Meg pointed her thumb to her chest. "I'm not a day o'er a hundred and fifty."

"What?" we all said at the same time.

"But," Thomas said, "you look so young."

Meg smiled. "Aye. In my world, we all look like this. Never age. For that matter, we don't do that strange thing you do in your world after someone lives too long. What's it called when a life comes to an end?"

"Die?" Dylan said, his voice skeptical.

Meg snapped her fingers. "Aye. That's it. Death from old age is a foreign idea."

"So you can't die?" Jade asked.

Meg chortled. "Nonsense. We can do that. Accidents can happen. But when we do, our spirits go to the Northern pond to dwell. Many good conversations you can have with those spirits."

I scratched my cheek. This was a bizarre concept. I exchanged looks with everyone.

Meg rose, put equipment away in duffel bags, and addressed us. "We should go. Ronan will be sending out patrols to find ya, if he hasn't already." She pointed down to the bag. "Grab that, would ya."

Jade and Dylan picked up the smaller ones and carried them over. I grabbed the handle to the larger and yanked on it, but it did not budge. I waved to Thomas, and he grabbed it with both hands. I gritted my teeth, and we dragged it to the sleigh. Meg stepped up, grabbed the heavy bag with one hand, lifted it with ease, and put it in the back.

"Did, uh, Witch Ruth give you that coin?" I asked, out of breath.

She turned to me. "It's a charm. And a complicated answer that one is. The answer is nay and yea. But I have to say, Witch Ruth ne'er gave me that charm directly. We Northerners have many magical charms like this." She knelt down in the snow and inspected the runners on the sleigh.

"Wait, so you've known Aunt—I mean Witch Ruth for a long time?" Dylan asked.

Meg stood up and stepped to the wolves, fixing the reins on each of them, and said, "Aye. Usually talk to her through a magic hologram. She has talked to us several times, she has. Her great-great-grandmother, though, helped us forge the magical gold charms long ago to protect our realm against Ronan."

Meg was up again and came back to the driver's seat of the sleigh. She waved for us to join her and sit in the back.

There were two rows of seats. We stepped up, and Thomas asked the question that was on all our minds. "Is Ronan completely mental? Why did he kidnap Erin? And what does the plonk want with Dylan?"

Meg pulled her hood over her head and picked up her reins. "If by mental you mean is he crazy, then yea, he is. Ya see, he thinks Erin and Dylan are his children who died years ago. He plans to raise them here."

She turned back around, held the reins up in her fists, then swung them down, yelling out, "Ha!" The sleigh jolted forward and gained speed. We headed onto the frozen river and wound around its curves. The trees were snow covered on either side of us and whisked by at eye-blinking speed.

After several moments, we departed the canyon of frozen trees and came out onto a vast plain of snow and ice. We were on the lake. The sky in front of us was overcast and dark and the air became colder.

A funnel of snow swirled toward us, and we hit it straight on. Ice pelted against my cheeks and face, and I closed my eyes. When the sensation disappeared, I opened them again. We had passed through it. The white tornado was now at our backs.

Dylan was looking over the side. Jade was curled up on her seat, hugging her knees. Thomas held a gloved hand up to his face, blocking some of the splatter of snow and slush.

I turned back around and stared at the silhouette of the castle on the peak of the mountain. It dawned on me that we were going straight into Ronan's hands and, by virtue of this, putting Dylan into Ronan's reach.

Chapter Eighteen

SHEETS OF SNOW flurries fell down over us. The mountain range drew closer, and we headed toward a large mountainous valley. We'd sped across the lake at what seemed to be breakneck speed, and I was surprised to see the mountainous terrain loom so large so quickly.

On occasion, the sled swayed over the layer of snow, and Meg shouted to her wolves. The sled skidded sideways for a moment, and a sheet of ice and wetness spewed over me. Within a few seconds, though, the sled straightened itself out.

Jade kept herself hunched down in her seat, but Thomas and Dylan were a bit more daring and peered over the sleigh's edge.

I had many questions rolling around in my head that I wanted to ask. The least was to find out how Ronan came to be. But the combination of the noisy wind and Meg being too busy driving our sled made it impossible to ask anything.

Dylan stared around frantically. He pushed his hood down, and his cheeks were rosy and eyes huge.

I leaned over and yelled over the wind, "What's wrong?"

He wiped the gleam of wetness from his face and replied in a loud voice. "Ronan. He's near."

Someone grabbed my shoulder, and Thomas shouted in my ear. *"Colton! We're blimey done for!"* He pointed his gloved hand forward. The valley was fast approaching, and I didn't see anything but slopes of white snow and rock on either side. There were a few rocks sliding down the incline.

I squinted. *No.*

Those weren't rocks sliding down the hill. They were white wolves. And they were thronged on the mountainous terrain and charging toward us.

I tapped Meg's back. Did she even see them?

She hollered back. "Hang on, small'ns. Might get a wee bit bumpy." She looked over her shoulder to me. "Take the reins."

"What?" I shouted.

She pushed me forward and shoved the reins into my hand. I gripped them hard. Her wolves' paws expelled a fine mist that sprayed over my face. Meg stood at my side and, having taken off her mittens, held gold coins in one bare hand. I looked out over the heads of the wolves pulling us and beyond. Two hundred feet in front of us, the landscape filled with a multitude of white wolves, too many to count. They stampeded straight at us.

"Meg!" I shouted. The gold coin glowed and then melted into her hand. She held both of her palms outward, and her hands became partially transparent. Flashes of light erupted from them, over and over. Bright yellow-bronze orbs streaked toward the large force of wolves and hit the front line. Plumes of pure white snow exploded in the air, one after the other. The sleigh flew through the whiteout, and my face was enveloped in a wet coldness. I clutched the reins hard, scared of letting them go, and ducked my head down. Ice and snow smacked loudly into my coat and hood. Wetness slapped my face. When it stopped, I looked up.

Behind me, the clouds of snow were still settling to the ground, but the wolves were gone.

"That was totally sweet!" Dylan shouted.

Thomas turned back to Meg and bleated, *"Ronan's wolves are bloody made of snow?"*

Meg took the reins from me. "Aye, they are. Ronan's dark sorcery. But let me assure ya, the wolves are real enough if they catch ya."

We bounded around the curve in the valley.

Dylan pointed up the hill. On both sides, white wolves careened toward us, meaning to intercept the sleigh. Meg held her hand up, and the same flashes of light ruptured from her hand, but it was not as intense as before. White radiating spheres flew forward, and the sides of the mountainous terrain exploded outward, causing columns of snow and dirt to rocket into the sky. I covered my face this time, not as timid as I had been before. Pebbles and clumps of snow landed on me, and then we were out from under the raining ice.

"More!" Jade yelled from behind us.

Meg turned. Several packs of white wolves came at our backs. Meg swung her reins down and yelled, "Ha!" The sled jolted, her wolves found renewed energy, and we spurted forward.

Thomas grabbed my arm and pointed, his mouth working. A squeak might have come out. A massive force of wolves was charging and about to collide with us. I grabbed the ledge in front of me and held my breath.

Meg didn't slow but instead spurred us forward. She shouted, "Ha! Ha!" The sled picked up more speed, and Meg turned us from the main valley road onto a new path I had not even seen coming. We raced over a slim road inside a narrow canyon. A rock face to one side and a drop on the other that plunged down to a frozen river. Meg turned and held her hand behind her. Two orbs flew out of her palm and hit where we had just entered. Rock detonated from each wall, boulders of all sizes tumbled down, and the entrance was sealed shut.

Over twenty white wolves emerged from the cloudy wreckage and sprinted after us over the narrow path.

"Meg!" I shouted and tugged on her sleeve.

She stared behind us and shook her head. "Rascally critters, aren't they?" She brought her hand out, and one small bright orb flew from her hand, zipped behind us and hit the lead wolf. It burst into a fine cloud of whiteness. She flexed her fingers, but nothing else happened. "Sorry, small'ns. I'm out." The pack of Ronan's wolves gained speed.

Meg handed me the reins again. "Take these." I took them, whipping them down on the poor beasts, but our wolves had lost steam and we were losing momentum.

Meg fiddled inside her satchel. "I should have a couple more charms. But saving one for ya."

I looked over my shoulder. Jade stood up and looked from Meg's wolves to the fiendish ones chasing us. She grabbed Dylan and shook him.

"We have our own charms. I don't think we can do what Meg did, but..." She pulled on her hair. Her face was drawn up in concentration. Her eyes flickered, and she held her finger up. "Got the image in my head." She shouted, "Realize avalanche!"

Out of nowhere, considerable rock debris tumbled down from up high on the mountain. It beelined toward the wolf pack. A hand made of rock rose from the sliding rocky barrage, and it clenched into a fist over the entire group of wolves. Snow sprayed out between the fingers. The avalanche destroyed the road, and boulders plummeted to the base of the cliff far below.

Our sled decreased speed and came to a stop. A few feet ahead was a footpath. The ground under us trembled, and I exhaled and put my gloves up to my face, amazed at what had transpired.

Dylan pumped his fist in the air. "Yes!"

Jade wore a smug grin.

Even Meg gawked out behind us. She held a couple of gold coins in her hand and turned to Jade, gave a half-cocked smile, and nodded. "Well done getting us in the clear, small'n." She held up her gold coin. "Can save these now."

Thomas squealed and jabbed his finger forward. "Not clear, not clear!"

I wheeled around. A mammoth seven-foot-tall werewolf was at our front, standing on its hind legs. It leered and showed off rows of sharp teeth.

Meg whispered, "Ronan."

Chapter Nineteen

RONAN'S GRIN, IF that was what it was, stretched from side to side and revealed razor-sharp teeth. He sauntered forward and held out one clawed hand. "Give him to me, and I'll let you live." He clearly meant Dylan.

"Hang onto something, small'ns. This is going to be more than a wee bumpy," Meg muttered in a low voice, then shook her head. "He is not yars, ya madman. Leave him alone. And give us Witch Ruth and the other small'n back. Ya have yar castle, and we have our North. Let everyone be, ya dark sorcerer."

Ronan howled into the air, and all of Meg's wolves cowered in their places. He dropped to all fours and charged straight at us.

Meg snapped her fingers, and the reins fell off her wolf pack. She gave a quick command, "Go!" The tired wolves did not need any additional prodding but fled from the sleigh. They headed to the nearby footpath that cut through the mountain and disappeared from the road we were on.

Ronan was close, and Meg raised her fist and brought it down. A fiery ball flew out from her knuckles and hit the ground in front of the sled. An explosion of blue light and the road under us was gone. The sleigh dropped through the newly made gap. Ronan flew over us, and I glanced up as he jumped to the other side of the breach. His claws clutched the ledge, and his body dangled down. He stared down at us in shock.

My stomach shot to my mouth and whirled in every direction. I gripped the side as the frozen river approached fast. Cold wind whipped my hood off, and my cheeks chilled.

Meg flicked her wrist, and an icy path popped up under us. The runners of the sleigh clanked down onto the new trail, which levitated in the air. We slid over the icy path without any way to steer. Meg snapped her wrist again, and the runners fit onto a track over the free-floating ice pathway.

The icy track went down at a steep angle, and the frozen river approached quickly. The angle plateaued to some degree, and Meg hollered, "Get ready to jump! Oy. Don't hold onto anything," she yelled. The sled took a hard turn, and my momentum carried me straight. I flew in the air, and in my terror, I observed Thomas's red hair, his hat twirling in the air. I flew face-first toward the ground, covered with rocks and snow. In one second, it transformed before my eyes to a huge snowdrift, and I plowed into it, eating snow. A harsh sound indicated the sleigh had crashed.

I crawled out of my cavern, tumbled down a side of the drift, and came to a stop at the bottom. Meg was getting up off her hands and knees, spitting out snow.

"Thank goodness I made that cushion at the last moment," she muttered.

I brushed the ice off my hat, and Dylan's head popped out of the drift, his hair and eyebrows covered in snow. He was laughing as he wiped off his face. "Way cool."

Jade burst from one side of the drift and rolled onto the ground, coughing up snow.

Thomas shrieked from inside the snowdrift. "Help!"

I took off my gloves, climbed up the packed snow, and reached inside where I thought I'd heard him. I clutched onto a shirt, and a fist tightened over mine. I yanked. Dylan and Jade pulled on my shoulder, and Thomas's head popped to the surface.

He spit slush from his mouth and grinned. "That was brilliant."

Meg came up, grabbed hold of Thomas, and hauled him out. "The devil will come down soon."

I stared up at the surreal-looking ice pathways that floated in the air. Water dripped from them, and I marveled once again at this magic.

She turned to the river and sighed. "We have to run for the bridge crossroads on foot. Oy, a long trek on foot. But that sleigh is done for."

I looked out to the middle of the river where the sleigh had been crushed on impact. Part of it had broken through the ice and sunk. A staccato series of bangs erupted as the sled broke through the surface and submerged into the frothy water.

"He doesn't know about the door, so we have time. But it's far, and we have to hurry." She pointed forward.

"What door? What crossroads?" Jade asked.

"It's at the Weredom Memorial," Meg said. "There, ya'll find a door. It'll take ya straight to Ronan's castle. Witch Ruth has made it so that you can go through."

"Wait, guys," Dylan said, flicking the snow from his bangs. "Let's just chill. I think I can get us there faster." He grinned and tapped his head. "Idea. Realize sleigh and reins!"

Pieces of the destroyed sled flew out of the river and assembled in front of us. In two blinks, a smaller sleigh than the one we had been riding on manifested.

"Oh, Dylan, great blimey idea. But who's going to pull us? Thomas?" Jade said.

I turned to Dylan, wondering the same thing. Dylan was not in sight, though.

Thomas rubbed his chin. "See? Chill means going to the loo."

Something rubbed against my leg, and I looked down at a black wolf. I flinched and stepped back. "Dylan?"

Dylan held his coat and clothes in his mouth. He dropped them near my feet, hurried away, and returned with his shoes, plopping them down too. Then he trotted to the sleigh.

Meg cawed. "Witch Ruth said ya could change into one. But this is wondrous news. I see why Ronan wants ya. Yar coat is silky just like his son."

Jade raised her eyebrows. "Ronan's son was a werewolf too?"

"Aye," Meg answered.

I picked up Dylan's clothes, threw them in the sled, and reached out to Dylan's snout, feeling stupid. He licked my fingers, and I petted his head.

"Why do Erin and Dylan look like his kids?" I asked Meg.

Meg came up to the sleigh, her hand sliding over the ledge as she admired it. She answered casually. "Well, Ronan is their great-great-great-great-granddad, o'course. Maybe ya could add a couple of greats in there."

"What!" Jade asked. "Erin is a werewolf too?"

Meg knelt and gripped a runner, testing its sturdiness. "Nay, small'n. She's no werewolf. Most of Ronan's children or their children or their children, for that matter, never were. Dylan is something special. It happens like this, skipping generations."

Meg stood back up. "Ya should go, small'ns." She fastened the reins to Dylan and patted inside the sled for us to sit. "I'll tell ya this. Long ago, Ronan and his sister were great magicians. They made a doorway to your world where they wanted to live."

"Why?" I asked.

Meg smiled. "Well, to grow up into adulthood. None of us can do that here."

"Blimey fruitcakes! What!" Thomas blurted out. "What bloody children want to grow into adulthood?"

Meg shrugged. "I have no answer for that. But go, they did. They left, and only they could open and close the door. So we thought they had left forever."

"But something happened," I said. "Ronan's children died. Ronan came back to use magic in the North to bring them back."

Meg nodded. "Aye. I guess we didn't know that if you experience death like you do in your world, it could cause such trauma. And we didn't know that growing into an adult made someone a more powerful magician. Ronan's powers were vast. He planned to use our magic ponds in the North for his purpose, but no good would come of it. Ya shall never bring the dead back.

"Ronan's sister came to our world to help. She became our queen. She had her own powers and helped us to design the charms to defend against Ronan. So Ronan was thwarted, and he built his castle far away from our Northern coast. The more ice and snow he has, the more powers he has. The land around him turned to snow and ice. He tried to time travel."

Dylan howled into the air, and Meg looked down at him. She furrowed her brow. "Ya need to go. I think Ronan's close."

"What happened?" Jade asked, leaning forward.

Thomas was clawing at his face with anticipation. "Did he go back to the time of dinosaurs and throw up his hands in defeat?"

"Or," I said, "end up going forward in time to the age of flying cars?"

Meg stepped away and shook her head. "Nay. Neither. Nothing happened. Instead, he only had a vision. He saw two children walking by his old house on Lowre Few Lane. They looked exactly like his children, or to his eyes they did. They were Dylan and Erin, o'course. He made two guardian wolves to sit by his house and wait for the day they'd come."

"Guardian wolves?" Thomas asked, a huge question mark on his face.

I slapped his arm. "The wolf statues, you plonk."

"Oh."

"Aye," Meg said. "And Ronan waited here where he can't age for the day Dylan and Erin happened by his house. Then when he saw them, he thrust his magic out into your world in the form of ice and snow so as to capture them."

A sharp crackle came from the river. A crack snaked out over the surface.

She waved to them. "Go, small'ns."

Jade knitted her brows in grave concern. "What about you?"

My heart beat fast too. I didn't want to leave Meg.

She pushed against the sleigh, and it jolted forward. We gained momentum as she pushed us and said between breaths, "Dylan is just one. You are three. You need to make fast time. It's simple logic, me small'ns."

She shoved us onto the frozen river. Dylan heaved with all his might, towing us forward.

Thomas, Jade, and I all looked behind at Meg, waving to us. The ice around her ruptured, and a figure with eight legs rose behind her. A spider made of ice. Two more emerged.

We rounded a bend, and Meg went out of sight.

Chapter Twenty

MY MOUTH HUNG open as I stared from the rear of the sleigh. Did I just see that? Ice spiders?

I kneeled in the back seat, my mind numb. The sleigh was flying over the snow, and a powdery cloud blew up behind us.

Jade shook my arm. "We have to go back!"

Thomas grabbed tufts of his hair. "Are you completely mental?" he squeaked. "We just saw spiders...made of ice. It don't get worse than that."

I was not sure what we should do. Figures scampered around the far corner and a group of ice spiders advanced in our direction. I swallowed. "Maybe we should just bloody run?"

Jade nodded. "Aye, maybe so." She turned around and shouted. "Dylan, we have company."

Dylan pushed his ears back, dipped his head, and pulled harder, and the sled picked up speed.

Thomas stood up partially and placed his hand to his forehead, staring into the distance. The river wound around the hill and came to a cliff where it dropped off. The area had several mountain peaks. A bridge spanned across one ledge to a summit. Three more bridges spanned out to different mountaintops. The bridges all crossed through, and at the point where they met, a monumental werewolf rock sculpture soared high up into the air.

"That must be the Weredom Memorial," Jade said.

I looked behind us. The horrid spider creatures were getting closer. I leaned forward. We could take the steep slope to get to the base of the bridge much faster.

"Cut through, Dylan," I hollered.

Dylan jerked his head up, veering off the flat surface and down the slope. The sleigh hit its front end, and for one second, we came to a stop. I rammed into the sleigh's side, and Dylan kept running. His reins snapped off. The sled came down on its runners, and it started its descent down the slope.

We picked up speed. The sled threatened to overrun Dylan, and the whites of his eyes showed. I gripped a rudimentary lever that turned the runners, and it vibrated in my hand. I pulled hard.

It was not going to be in time. Dylan leaped to the left onto the surface of a fallen tree, and we started to speed past him. He vaulted into the air and landed on top of Thomas, taking him to the floor. I breathed in relief. Jagged rocks were straight ahead. I pulled on the lever again, and the runners barely turned. We skimmed over the lethal rocks, and sparks spewed into the air.

Up close, the bridge was wide, and we clearly had plenty of room. Except that the sled careened to the right side of the bridge, toward the edge of a cliff. Jade screamed behind me. I yanked on the lever, and the sleigh turned a couple of degrees. The front end aligned to the bridge. I sighed, thankful for small blessings.

Thomas was tapping my shoulder. "*Coltonnnnn...*"

I looked around, and three ice spiders were at our backs. One swung out its spindly leg made of crystal. It meant to sweep us off. Jade and Thomas ducked and fell on top of Dylan who was barking at the creature. I hunkered down, and the arm sliced over my head. My back hit the control lever, and I whirled around in time to see us veer toward a boulder. The sled's runners slammed into jagged stone, and we spun uncontrollably. We came onto the bridge's icy surface, hit the girder, and bounced off it. A hole appeared where we had hit the guardrail.

The spiders scampered over the bridge toward us. They all went into a slide on the slick surface, and one flew off into the gaping hole in the railing.

This was worse than any amusement ride. I was shoved up against the sleigh's side and unable to stand as we whirled around in circles.

The sled spun through the Weredom Memorial sculpture's legs, a sharp glimmer of blue sparkled, and we entered another snowy terrain with a dark, gloomy sky. I looked back at the doorway we had entered where the spiders attempted to come through but were shattered into tiny pieces of ice.

The sled did not stop its spin, making me sick to my stomach. We rose between walls, and it crashed into one. Wood splintered, pieces of debris littered behind us. We smacked into the other side, and I fell back on top of everyone else.

I came up to my knees, peeked over the top. We were about to head over yet another precipice. Ronan's castle loomed directly ahead and was, in fact, below us. I ducked down. Jade braced on her hands and knees, her eyes wide with horror.

"*Stay down,*" I yelled.

Then we were in the air. Jade fell on her stomach and hugged me. Thomas lay on his side, hugging Dylan and hiding his face in Dylan's shaggy coat. We descended, and the runners crashed back onto an icy terrain with a teeth-shattering jolt.

We flew downhill, and I took my arms off Jade. We both came up to stare over the ledge. The tattered sled slammed into a snowdrift, and a white blanket exploded into the air and showered down. The sleigh was only slowed by this obstacle. The runners hit the icy lake, and we skidded forward.

Dylan put his forepaws up to peer over the ledge. Thomas poked his head between Jade's and mine. We advanced past the middle of the lake. Our momentum thankfully slowed even more, and I determined I would tell my parents to cross off all future trips to amusement parks from my list.

The sleigh came to a standstill.

Jade slouched onto the floor. "Oy, thank goodness that's over."

I put my forehead in my hands and caught my breath. Thomas sat back onto the floor, his back against the seat, and his eyes squinted shut, asking, "Are the ice spiders gone?"

"Yes, Thomas," Jade answered.

"Be bloody thankful they have gravity here in Weredom. Otherwise, we never would have stopped," I said.

I stared up to the crystal spires of the castle. "Right, we made it to Ronan's castle. Dylan, where did your aunt say to go?" I looked to where Jade sat and back to Thomas who was pulling on his lips in some type of daze. "Oy, where'd Dylan go now?"

Dylan popped up from the very back seat in human form, wearing his shirt and pants. "Wha's up."

I pointed down. "You, uh, might want to close the barn door."

He looked down and chuckled. "Oopsies." He zipped his pants.

Dylan put on his coat and leaped over the back onto the ice. I stepped out of the sled and noticed a glint of metal on the ground. I bent over and picked up the coin. Meg had been saving us one, and she must have dropped it.

"We came from that?" Thomas declared in a high-pitched voice.

I gazed in the direction we had come. A steep mountainous terrain was in view. I brought my head up and was horrified we had come down such a treacherous incline. On the peak, thick barricades wrapped around a ridge that bordered the lake.

"Is that...is that a maze?" Jade asked.

I studied the terrain below. I turned and saw past the lake. Where the elevation decreased, there was indeed a maze. It appeared to wrap completely around the castle and went on as far as the eyes could see, disappearing into a fog.

I nodded.

"G-good thing the doorway took us to the end rather than the middle of that thing."

Dylan spoke from the back. "And the door took us close to a bridge that appears to go directly into the castle."

Jade, Thomas, and I all wheeled around to admire the colossal structure.

"Crikey, but it's big," Thomas observed dryly.

On the far side of the lake was a ridge and then a canyon that went between the plateau we were standing on and the castle. A covered parapet walk stretched over the gap. Along the castle wall in front of us were several tall towers with turrets on top.

Jade spoke. "Aunt Ruth said a tower. But which one?"

Dylan pointed. "Um, yeah, the black tower."

One corner tower was black.

The ice crackled around and behind us. We all exchanged looks and started to run but stopped short. A fissure broke in a circle around us, and water splashed up. Ice spiders formed one after the other. There were too many to count, circling around us. We huddled together, our backs pressed up against one another, and stared at the crazy, macabre spiders.

We all now stood on an island of ice with the ice spiders poised on the edge. Behind them was a large space of water. No one could make that leap across. If we could get past the defense line, we would have to swim through freezing water.

"I-it's blocked this way," I stammered.

"N-not good here, either," Jade said.

"It's a dead end over here too," Dylan said.

Thomas squeaked.

I licked my lips, remembered Ms. Griffin's words, and muttered, "Ice spiders can't skate."

I touched my coin in my pocket. I had to use it. But my mind was blank. I had no clue what to do.

Thomas whispered with utter realization, "Skate." I recalled Thomas had never used his last charm. He straightened and held up his finger. "Realize Ice Hockey arena."

A large portion of the sled vanished, the runners were gone, and a whirlwind of ice flew over the ice spiders, but they were dug in and couldn't be moved. The ring of water in the icy lake surface was gone. Ice skates materialized on my feet and a wooden hockey stick in my hand.

Dylan skated a circle around me and said, in high spirits, "Cool."

The ice spiders now all had skates made of a slick glazed ice that had replaced the pointed tips on the end of their legs. Their legs flew out side to side, and one tipped over, crashed, and smashed into pieces. Another one tumbled and turned into ruins.

Thomas pushed with one leg, then the other, and gained momentum in a quick fashion. He glanced back at us, grinning. "Follow me, fellas."

I attempted to mimic Thomas, but I was clumsy. Jade was beside me, even more unstable than I was. We grabbed hands to steady each other and both made a slow advance forward. Dylan spurred ahead and gave out a gleeful, boyish giggle. Dylan was, of course, a natural ice skater. I knew I shouldn't be surprised.

An ice spider moved to attack Thomas, but it glided to his side, out of control. Thomas swung his stick and disintegrated the end of the leg. The creature nosedived and fractured before my eyes. Chunks of ice belched out over the slick surface.

Thomas went to a knee and glided under the legs of another one. The spider tried to turn back to Thomas, but it was sliding uncontrollably, and it slipped toward Jade and I. We both pushed against each other and parted ways. Jade brought her hockey stick back, and I did too. We met eyes and swung at the same time as the multilegged thing passed between us. I was rewarded with a loud *crunch*. The frozen monster toppled to the ground and became ice chips.

Dylan smashed two legs of one spider, and it pirouetted, flying past me. I glanced over my shoulder. It collided with the eight-legged creatures coming from behind us, and large particles of ice exploded up into the air. The debris tripped others, and there was the dull sound of thumps as the ice spiders broke into fragments over the surface.

The enemies in front of Jade and me had thinned out, and I grabbed her hand and pushed forward. When we reached the end of the lake, I sat down on my butt and immediately started to remove my skates.

Dylan and Thomas were having fun and skating around the graceless spiders, amputating spindly ice legs one after the other. Dylan fell down and spun on his back toward one ice creature with legs that had been broken at the end. The blunt ends of the spider's legs stabilized it, and it rose up, meaning to crush Dylan.

I rose up. "No!" I ran out over the ice.

Jade grabbed my hand, and I jerked to a stop. "Wait, look."

Thomas had pivoted several feet away and brought his hockey stick back with both hands. He swung down hard at a chunk of ice close to his feet. There was a sharp crack. The chunk soared through the air straight to the ice spider's belly, and on impact, the creature broke into fragments.

Thomas skated over to Dylan, gripped his hand, and helped him up. Dylan headed toward me, his eyes large but a grin on his face. He held his thumb up and gave out a short laugh. I plopped back down on my butt, tried to smile, and held up a shaky thumb.

Jade leaned her head on my arm. "Who knew Thomas's hockey skills would save our lives?"

I nodded. "Aye. I'm absolutely gobsmacked."

Thomas skated toward us, made a quick stop, and slid several ice chunks in front of him. He hit them one after the other, destroying the remaining survivors until there was nothing but a rubble of broken-up ice lying over the frozen surface.

Chapter Twenty-One

I STEPPED OVER the snowy ridge, my nerves hyperalert. Any second, I expected something to attack, but it was eerily quiet. Dylan, Thomas, and Jade were right behind me. Something small and white flittered up off the icy ground and twirled in the air.

"Is that a butterfly?" Jade asked.

Thomas held his hand up, and the tiny winged creature landed on the tip of his thumb.

Dylan peered down at it. "I don't know. A moth? That's weird, huh? Living here in the cold and everything."

Jade pointed toward a pile of boulders. "There's more." Several white moths made lazy circles above the rocky terrain. A larger swarm of butterflies, or moths, or whatever they were, rose from the ground. Strange.

I reached the covered parapet and studied it. It looked sturdy enough. Designed of thick ice, it had windows along the walkway. I stepped to the cliff edge, close to where the bridge connected to land, and peeked over the ledge. No bottom was in sight, only a misty fog.

Thomas sneezed, and I jumped. Dylan grabbed my shoulder and pulled me back. I fell back into him and looked up to his face. He offered a crooked smile and patted my back.

"Be careful, dude. It'd not be cool to make it this far just for one of us to go splat."

I nodded. "R-right."

Dylan winked at me. "I'll go first." He started across the bridge, and I followed him.

"Colton, you still have the coin?" Jade asked.

"Meg said it was a charm," Thomas said.

"Okay, brilliant," Jade's tone was peeved. "*Charm*. Do you have it?"

I felt inside my pocket, my fingers closing over something hard. I brought it out and looked at it.

"Do you think Meg is okay?" Thomas asked.

I remembered the ice spiders forming around Meg. My heart ached, and I shook my head. I had no answer to that question.

"M-maybe she got away. They didn't want her," Jade said.

Dylan stopped in front of me, and we all froze in place. He turned and brought his finger up, whispering, "I smell him. He's somewhere inside this place."

I put the charm back in my pocket, leaned forward, and spoke in a hushed voice. "Ronan?"

Dylan nodded.

Thomas pulled on my sleeve. "Colton."

A sharp reply almost blurted out of my mouth, but I remembered Thomas had just saved our lives. Maybe it was time I gave Thomas more patience. I turned to him and raised my eyebrows. He pointed behind us, and I looked back and straightened.

A massive number of white moths had followed us inside the covered bridge and were on the windowsills, walls, ceilings. Others flew in random directions in front of us.

"W-we're going to be bloody grub. They're going to devour us," Thomas bleated.

I put my hand on his shoulder and shook my head. "No, I don't think so."

The tiny winged creatures resting on surfaces flew up and joined the ones already in the air, and a low, buzzing became audible. Their random directions turned into a pattern, and they spiraled, transforming into a pure white figure standing in front of us. It was a woman.

She fixed her hair and spoke. Aunt Ruth's voice came from the strange apparition. "Dylan, kids, can you hear me?"

I took a step back and bumped into the cold wall.

Dylan cocked his head to the side and squeaked, "Aunt Ruth? W-what... H-how?"

Aunt Ruth put her hands on her hips. "Yes, dear, it's me. Do you children have the coin?"

I nodded.

Thomas bumped my shoulder and used my own words on me. "She can't hear a bloody nod."

"We do," Jade answered.

Aunt Ruth nodded. I wasn't certain, but I thought she frowned. "I have dire news. I tried to take a charm from Ronan's chambers and was caught. Now, I'm frozen. This here is my consciousness, so to speak." She leaned forward and wagged her finger. "I was able to hide Erin. I'll show you where to go. The charm you have has only so much power, and you will need to use it to get to the portal and leave."

Dylan shook his head. "No, nooo. We can't leave you..."

Aunt Ruth held her hands up, gesturing for him to be quiet. "No time to argue. Leave me here. And when the time comes, I will chant a spell, and the door will be locked from both sides—I hope for good. Also, you will need to be cloaked invisible."

She raised her fingers, and a flock of moths surged out from her palm. They gyrated around me, and I shielded my face. My arms and chest and body were blanketed in white moths. I looked up. I didn't see anyone around me on the bridge. I looked down, and my body was gone.

Thomas's horrified voice spoke close to me. "They gobbled everyone up! And where's my bloody hands?"

"Thomas?" Jade's voice came from the darkness.

"Who's that?" Thomas answered.

"Jade, you clonk!"

"Oh, cool," Dylan said by my side. "I can't see anyone."

A funnel of moths rotated at a fast speed in front of me, and Aunt Ruth was back. She touched her chin and nodded.

"Not bad. It will not last that long. Oh, here, this will make it so you can see each other." She snapped her moth-made fingers, and my body returned. Dylan, Jade, and Thomas were in front of me.

Thomas gaped at his hands, grinning from ear to ear. A high-pitched laugh erupted from him.

Aunt Ruth started down the hall, speaking over her shoulder. "They can't see you, but they can hear you! Quiet." I slapped the back of Thomas's head. He rubbed where I hit him and gave me a sour face. I put my finger up to my mouth.

Aunt Ruth stepped to the end of the bridge, which led into a large, spacious foyer. She turned around, her eyes opened wide. "For all your sakes. Silence."

The moths swarmed everywhere and were camouflaged along the wall. I stepped close to the baluster and spied around the edge. A force of white wolves trotted toward me, and I brought my head back.

Everyone stared at me.

"What is it?" Jade asked in a quiet voice.

Dylan peeked around and popped his head back quick. "Wolves. Let's hope this cloak thing works."

I held my breath. The troop moved past our pillar, and Thomas crinkled his nose as if he was about to sneeze. My finger flew up and went under his nose. His hands came up over mine, and his eyes fluttered. The large group moved past us and went down a long corridor that had half-moon shaped walls. A few stragglers passed by.

I sighed in relief and started to step out. Dylan pushed on my chest and shook his head. I then heard the loud scraping noise. The source of the sound became obvious. A group of wolves came into view, pulling a rectangular block of ice behind them. A person was inside that frozen brick.

Jade grabbed my wrist. Thomas brought his hands down, his eyes huge. I shook my head in despair.

"No," Dylan whispered.

Meg was inside the icy slab with her mouth open wide. She had one hand raised up, and between her fingers, she held a gold coin. Icicles were formed over it.

Thomas let out a sneeze. I gritted my teeth and looked over at the wolves hauling Meg. They stopped and looked around them. One stared directly at me and then swiveled its head to scan the area.

Clanking approached, and I hugged my chest. Three seconds ticked by. Ronan's two stone guardian wolves stepped up, and one swiveled its head toward us. Its red eyes radiated. The guardian wolf didn't see any of us, turned to continue forward, and let out a growl. The white wolves hauled Meg away.

We waited for several moments, and the orb reappeared in front of us.

"We have to save Meg," Jade whispered.

Dylan shook his head. "You heard what Aunt Ruth said. We can't."

I nodded. "Jade. Bloody sake. Come on. We can't blather about it right here. We'll get caught."

Tears welled up in her eyes. Thomas looked between her and me. She wiped the corner of her eyes and nodded. "Okay. Let's go."

Chapter Twenty-Two

AUNT RUTH LED us down the long half-circle hallway that made a long curve to the left. On the corridor side, ice sculptures the same size as me portrayed a boy and a girl in different poses that ranged in variety from waving, rubbing a chin with a furrowed brow, or wagging a finger. The children resembled Erin and Dylan, and I surmised these statues must have been made in the likenesses of Ronan's children. Our footfalls echoed through the corridor, and a sense of desolation and despair filled me. The statues were the only memories Ronan had of his children.

We snaked around a couple of bends, and Aunt Ruth stopped at an open window. Crystal-clear ice formed the windowpane, and I stared down at a courtyard. Multiple ice sculptures of Ronan's son and daughter were spread over the plaza, completing various actions with one another. In one, they had their hands laced together, while another had them sitting together, and yet another pair had them holding each other's hands while leaning back, appearing to spin in a circle. In the square center were two larger sculptures of Ronan's son and daughter. At the base of these ice statues knelt Ronan, his head hung down, and one of his hands splayed on the leg of the girl. Weeping reached us, and my shoulders sagged. Even after all these years, Ronan still mourned the loss of his children. Dylan, Jade, and Thomas looked out the window and did not speak a word. Jade wiped wetness from her cheek, and Dylan and Thomas had mopey faces.

Aunt Ruth tapped my shoulder and waved for me to follow. I hissed at the others, and they glanced in my direction and we all went. After two more bends, Aunt Ruth reached a wide archway. I came up close to her and peeked into the room. Dylan, Jade, and Thomas peered around me as well.

It was a great hall with a long table in the middle. The white wolves sat on the ground, some up on ledges, and others milled around. Close to the doorway were too many wolves to count. I had no idea how we could move through this room. We would surely step on one!

Jade jabbed her finger across the room. On the far side of the room, the frozen slab containing Meg stood up on its end. Her glazed eyes stared out at us. Next to her was another slab of ice that contained a person. I swallowed. Aunt Ruth.

I came back around the corner, and everyone huddled close to me. Aunt Ruth's moth figure hunched down and spoke with a feathery voice.

"You're almost there. To the far corner, there's a door with the werewolf warrior figurine. The charm will let you into the room I created."

Thomas furrowed his brow. "The room you created?"

Aunt Ruth put her finger over Thomas's mouth, and his eyes enlarged. She shook her head. "Silence that tongue, lad."

She took her hand away from Thomas, and a moth flittered up in the air from Aunt Ruth's fingers to settle on the end of Thomas's nose. Both his eyes pointed at the moth, but his mouth remained sealed shut.

Aunt Ruth wagged her finger back and forth to us. "Ronan is near. Now, when I make the distraction, get to the other side. Not before."

Dylan reached out to Aunt Ruth and said in a hushed voice, "Wait. Aunt Ruth." His fingers slipped through hers, though.

She gazed down at him, and he stared at his hand in surprise. A couple of moths were on the tips of his fingers, and he shook them off. "What's the distraction?"

She winked. "You'll know."

The moths blew up into a swarm, swirled around me, and I covered my head. The horde passed through the door, and I looked out into the room. The moths gyrated around the wolves and spooked them, and several bit at the air and managed to swallow some. But there were too many, and the wolves backed away into the middle of the room.

"I guess that's the distraction she was talking about," Jade whispered.

Dylan pointed. "There."

Not far from the door we needed was a seven-foot-tall werewolf warrior ice sculpture that held an ice axe at its side.

I turned to Thomas and held my finger up. "Don't you dare sneeze."

Thomas saluted and made like he was locking his mouth with a key.

We made it to the doorway near a base to a spiraling staircase. Then Thomas knocked into the sculpture by the door, and it began to tip over. Dylan and Jade put their hands up and balanced it. The axe fell forward, though, and I watched its descent helplessly. Thomas knelt quickly, and I was amazed at his speed and that he caught it before it smashed over the floor. A couple of nearby wolves were staring at the axe. Their hackles raised. They no doubt saw an axe floating in the air.

I grabbed Thomas's collar and yanked him out of the large chamber. He was up to his feet and brought the axe with him, and we stood at the base of a spiraling staircase.

I stared at Thomas and his axe. "Thomas, you clonk. What are you going to do with that?"

Thomas stared down at the weapon in his hands and shrugged. "Should I put it back?"

Dylan and Jade had climbed a few steps and said simultaneously, "No!"

Dylan held up his hands. "It's cool. Keep it." He gave Thomas a thumbs-up and offered a nervous smile.

Aunt Ruth's voice spoke from above us at a bend in the staircase. She pointed behind me. "Children. You have company."

Two wolves had come from the chamber room toward the stairwell and swiveled their heads. One stared straight at Jade, the other at Dylan, and snarled.

Jade spoke with her lips closed. "I think they see me?"

"The invisibility cloak has worn off," Aunt Ruth said.

She held out her hand, and a small swarm of moths flew to Thomas, gyrating around his weapon and melding into it.

Two more wolves came inside, stared at all of us, and crept forward.

"We need to run," Dylan said.

"Use the weapon, child, before it's too late," Aunt Ruth said.

Thomas balked, looked down at the axe, and stepped up. There were bright flashes from the end of his axe. Balls of fiery light flew out to hit the wolves, and they turned into powdery snow. Thomas held the axe straight out from him, his eyes wide with amazement.

"It's been enchanted, and we're reaching the last of my magic. Let's hope this one lasts longer than the cloak. Follow me," Aunt Ruth said.

Two more bends and Aunt Ruth stopped. She put a hand on the wall. "Bring out the charm."

I fished the coin out from my pocket, holding it up in my palm, and Aunt Ruth tapped its surface. It glowed, rose in the air, and glided to the wall. A bright light flashed, and there was an opened doorway in front of us. The bright orb floated back to my open hand and was a coin again. I tucked it in my pocket and was through the doorway. The others followed me inside.

Erin was sitting on the side of the wall staring out of a window overlooking the icy kingdom. The vast maze surrounding the castle was clear. The room had nice furniture, a fireplace, books on a shelf, a bathroom, and even stovetops and cabinets. I guessed if someone were trapped in an ice castle, it was the best place to hide.

Erin shot to her feet, gave out a cry of surprise, and stared at us with her mouth wide open.

"Heya, Erin," Jade said from beside me.

Erin licked her lips. "Jade?" She turned to me. "Colton?" Then Thomas and Dylan. "W-what... how?"

Dylan stepped forward. "Long story. We probably shouldn't chat too long. Apparently, a crazy man named Ronan wants to raise us like his own children."

Erin started to sob and hurried to the open doorway, muttering, "We have to go. T-the loony man will find us."

She stopped in the doorway, looking out into the stairwell with humongous eyes. Her hand flew to her mouth, and she stumbled backward. Three wolves hurried toward Erin, and Thomas stepped in front and shielded her. He held up his axe, and fiery balls flew out. Watery slush pooled on the ground.

Thomas craned his neck and turned to Erin, who hugged her chest and stared at the powdery snow on the ground. He patted her arm. "Don't worry, lass. You're safe with me." He turned to us. "Think I could get used to this."

A funnel of moths swirled to the middle of the room, and Aunt Ruth stood front and center. Erin's eyes rolled back, and she fainted. Thomas caught her with one arm and crouched down with her.

Aunt Ruth looked down at her, sighed, and held her hands up. "You will need to wake her. I'll guide you back outside and take you through the maze. Dylan, get that lass awake. We don't have much time."

I dug in my pocket and brought out the gold coin, considering it. "Wait."

Aunt Ruth winced at that remark and fixed her gaze on me. Dylan, Jade, and Thomas turned toward me.

"Meg has a coin in her hand. We free her with this one, and then we have a new one," I said.

A smirk formed on Dylan's face. "Nice, dude."

Jade and Thomas nodded.

"Children, enough of your blathering. Don't think I didn't think of it. It's too dangerous. Now, it's time to go—" Aunt Ruth said.

Dylan stomped his foot, and his face reddened. "Aunt Ruth! Please! We're trying to talk!"

Aunt Ruth's mouth fell open. "Young sir, how dare you speak to me like that!"

She put her hands on her hips. It was an amusing sight. A few moths flapped around overhead, a couple dipping in and out from her shoulder.

She shook her finger back and forth. "I'll not have my child nephew speak..."

Dylan held up his palm, cutting her off. "Aunt, give it a rest! Can't you see we're trying to save you? Now, I know I'm only a kid, but just trust me and let me figure things out." He pointed his finger up. "So, if you don't mind, keep your mothball lips sealed. Let the kids chat."

Aunt Ruth crossed her arms and looked up to the ceiling.

Dylan rubbed the back of his neck and looked to us. "Sorry about that." He turned to me. "What's your idea?"

Chapter Twenty-Three

I TOOK A deep breath and stared out the doorway into the great hall. The white wolves were all calm. I turned back to everyone and met their eyes. "You ready?"

Dylan gave me two thumbs up. "Born ready, dude."

"Born ready?" I furrowed my brow, shook my head, and turned to Jade.

She nodded.

Thomas had eager anticipation on his face and gave one quick nod.

Erin leaned on Thomas, her eyes a bit unfocused. "W-what are you doing?" She peered into the chamber with the large force of wolves. "T-they'll eat us."

Thomas patted her back and said, "Don't worry, lass. We know magic."

Erin furrowed her brow. "Magic?"

I reached out and touched Erin's hand. She startled at that and stared at me.

"Look. I'm sorry for saying those mean things I said. But we really can do magic, and we can escape. You want to leave, right?"

Erin looked at me with big fish eyes and vigorously nodded.

I held my finger up to my mouth. "Okay, then. Just do what we say, okay?"

Another nod of consent.

I looked up to Aunt Ruth who stood above on the stairs, her arms crossed over her chest, emanating her peevishness.

"Aunt Ruth, you ready?" I asked.

Aunt Ruth didn't look at me but up into the air. "Oh, sure. I'm ready to watch you children walk into a wolf's den. Not to mention Werewolf Ronan not too far away. Sounds quite delightful. Can't wait to see you all captured."

I held up the coin in my hand. "So how do we, uh, make the blimey thing work?"

Aunt Ruth sighed. "Remember, you just get one desire each. Part of its energy has been used." She put out her hand and moths, fluttering in the air, twirled down to my palm. The coin glowed, hovered in the air, and then four fireballs split from the radiating orb and streaked into Dylan, Jade, Thomas, and me. No one thought Erin was up to it yet.

I stepped out of the room, and Jade came to my side. Wolves bolted to their feet in alarm at our sudden appearance.

"Realize wooden buckets," I said.

The long wooden table in the middle of the room vanished, and three large wooden buckets formed in front of the ice slabs of Meg and Aunt Ruth.

"Thomas, Dylan. Go," Jade said.

Dylan and Thomas ran toward the slabs of ice. Fireballs flew out of Thomas's axe, and clouds of fine powdery snow swirled where the white wolves had stood.

Jade and I rushed forward, and I tugged on Erin's hand. A swarm of moths flew around us giving what aide they could.

"Realize anchors!" Jade yelled. The iron chandelier vanished. The blue crystals fell and smashed on the ground. Three iron anchors attached themselves to the wooden buckets.

Thomas and Dylan had reached the ice block with Meg. Thomas set his axe down and helped Dylan tip Meg's ice cube so it fell headfirst into the bucket. Jade and I reached Aunt Ruth's slab and shoved it. It toppled forward and slanted inside the second bucket.

Wolves charged. Thomas picked up his axe, and bright flashes of light spurted from the axe end. The air was filled with a white sheet of exploding snow, and my face was misted. I got into the third empty bucket and pulled Erin inside. Dylan and Jade got in next.

All the moths swooped in on the attacking wolves.

"Get in, Thomas!"

Thomas stuck a leg over and got inside, his axe held firm in both hands.

I punched his arm. "Say it."

"Oh, realize flood!"

The walls around us melted, and I ducked down and yelled, "Hang on!"

A flash flood erupted and a torrent surged, around and over us. I held my breath. I peeked over the ledge, my clothes soaked. The deluge swept the wolf force away and tunneled through different corridors.

I rose to my feet. The entire room glistened a slick white. It was completely bare except for our buckets.

We got out, drenched and shivering. I looked at everyone and nodded to Dylan.

Dylan stood over the buckets with Meg and Aunt Ruth's slabs. They were full of water too.

"Realize burning fire," he said.

The two wooden buckets transformed, and iron bottoms formed. The ice slabs flipped in the air, then back inside, feetfirst. A large fiery globe glided from the door where Erin had been and came across the room. Within a blink, it was under the two buckets and three bright fires burned. My clothes were off me in an instant, and I barely knew I was naked when dry clothes appeared back on my body.

"Thanks to Aunt Ruth for her fire upstairs," Jade said, patting her dry coat with her hand.

"W-where did the, uh, moth Aunt Ruth go?" Erin stammered.

I looked around. "I guess the poor buggers got washed away."

A moan sounded behind me, and I turned. Meg was inside her bucket, steam rising from the surface, a few patches of ice still on her.

"I tell ya. Those ice spiders are tricky creatures."

Jade jumped up and down. I looked over to Aunt Ruth who, as a bigger person, had yet to be unfrozen. The top portion of her was still covered in ice. I leaned in closer. In one fist, she held a gold coin that was half visible and not covered by any ice. Aunt Ruth must have managed to get a charm from Ronan's chambers before she was caught.

"No," Dylan groaned,

I turned to him. "What?"

"He's here."

I wheeled around. A dark shadow moved from an archway across the room and a mammoth-sized person stepped toward us, a hood over his head. Stone wolves flanked him on each side. Their eyes were a fiendish crimson red. One carried a net that gleamed silver in its mouth.

"No," I whispered.

Ronan pushed his hood back and smiled. "Aye. You are all here then." He turned to Dylan and bowed. "I thought you would come for your aunt. I considered trying to bring you here. Your home was so close. But your aunt would meddle. Well, now you are home." Then to Erin. "You both will be happy here. Maybe not at first. But in time. You'll see."

"Ronan, ya crazy yobo," Meg said. "They're just children. And they're not yours, ya madman."

Ronan snarled and muttered, "Take them."

The stone wolf that was holding a silver net in its mouth jerked its head, and the net flew through the air and fell on top of Dylan.

Dylan crumpled to his knees and groaned in pain.

"Dylan," I screamed.

Thomas pointed his axe, and a series of light flashes flew out toward Ronan. Both stone wolves vaulted in the air and absorbed the hits, landing several feet in front of us. They crouched low to the ground, about to spring again. Ronan flicked his hand. The axe shattered in Thomas's hand, and the fires under the buckets snuffed out.

Ronan thrust out his palm to Meg. The water in Meg's bucket froze in a second and icicles formed over Meg's body once again. Her fist tightened over the charm in her hand and her hand glowed. The ice turned back to water.

"Dylan. If ya don't mind, we need ya in the other form when that net's off ya. We're making a dash for it, we are," she said.

She thrust her hand out, and there was a bright flash. I put my face in my hands, tiny dots in my eyes.

I realized I was sitting down in something, and it was moving. My vision returned. I was once again in a sleigh— no, a bobsled. Jade was in front of me, and then Thomas, and the front seat was empty except for Dylan's coat and clothes. Dylan was in werewolf form and pulling us forward. I looked over my shoulder, getting my bearings. A second bobsled was hitched to us. In the front seat was Meg, and then Erin, and behind her was Aunt Ruth, the top half of her still frozen.

I stared forward again. Part of the great hall had been drastically changed. The walls in front were gone, and I could view outside. We were headed toward a straightaway track that made a few curves with steep banks and ended near the edge of the lake. Dylan pulled toward the mouth of the slide.

Ronan had fallen to his knees. His wrists had silver cuffs fastened over them with silver-chain links staked to the ground. The stone wolves had wooden cuffs over their legs.

The wolves broke free and barreled forward. Ronan bared his teeth, and his body changed into a mammoth werewolf. He pulled his arms forward, and the chains snapped.

Then he was out of my vision. The bobsled tipped down and started its slide. Meg snapped her fingers, and the reins fell off Dylan's neck. He leaped onto the side of the wall and into the front seat. I glanced over my shoulder as the air whipped over my ears. Meg's bobsled had detached from us.

I gripped the sides for my life. For the umpteenth time in the last two days, my stomach somersaulted and I wanted to vomit.

I closed my eyes as Thomas yelled, "*Woo-hoo!*"

I really never wanted to go on another roller coaster, slide, merry-go-round, or even a swing. Nothing. Ever.

Chapter Twenty-Four

THE BOBSLED CAME to the bottom of the track and skimmed over the lake's iced surface. It turned until we were sideways. Meg's bobsled zoomed straight, broadsiding us. We continued to rotate in circles until we came to the edge of the lake where there were snowdrifts, which brought us to an abrupt stop. I scrambled out over the side. Dylan had changed back to human form, donned clothes, and was pulling on his coat.

Meg's bobsled came to a sudden stop close to ours and tipped a bit to the side. Aunt Ruth's slab of ice fell and flipped so she was standing on her head now in her ice cube. Meg jumped out a second later, grabbed Erin, and pulled her down before putting her hands on the top portion of Aunt Ruth's frozenness. Steam rose between her fingers and rivulets of water streamed down. Within a few seconds, Aunt Ruth was unfrozen, and Meg let her gently lower to the ground. Meg put her ear to Aunt Ruth's chest. The gold coin rolled from Aunt Ruth's fingers, curving toward me, and I bent down and picked it up.

"I hear a beating heart. It'll take a while until she awakens." Meg looked to my hand. "'Tis fortunate we have one left. Save it for the portal."

"*They're coming!*" Jade shouted.

A stone statue wolf came skating down the bobsled track, sitting back on its haunches. Its red eyes were enormous, and its forepaws pressed forward, its claws thrust into the icy ground, trying to slow its descent. It came off the slide and went into three-hundred-and-sixty-degree turns, zooming over the ice. A second one flew down at its back. Ronan came next in his massive hairy beast form, and he, too, looked uncoordinated and careened out of control.

The lake was huge, and wherever we had landed the first time must have been far away. Here, there was no ridge we had to ascend, but flat ground, and the maze was a hundred feet away, an entrance in view.

"Run, children! Into the maze! I'll catch up," Meg shouted.

I pulled on Erin's hand and turned to see if we were being pursued. One statue came to its feet, looking wobbly. Jade was on my heels, and Dylan hesitated. He looked back to Meg, who had managed to form a gurney that held the sleeping Aunt Ruth. Two wooden handles stuck out of the end, and Meg held onto these as she pulled her forward.

"Go! We need to get to the temple sanctum. The portal doorway is there," she yelled to us.

The ice over the lake behind us cracked, water splashed up, and a multitude of huge ice spiders clambered in our direction. Ronan stood, his clawed fists at his side, and stared with bright crystal-blue eyes.

"Dylan, come on!" I said.

Dylan turned and ran after me, and we headed toward a wide entryway leading into the maze. Snow funnels twisted close by us, and white wolves manifested.

I sped through the opening and let Erin go, saying, "Stay close."

She nodded, her eyes terrified.

Thomas came through the entry and leaned an arm on the wall, breathing hard and muttering, "Bloody sakes. That's a lot of wolves and ice spiders..."

Jade and Dylan entered next. Meg was right behind them.

I stared at the three doorways in front of us. "Which way?"

Dylan stepped ahead of me. "This way. I can smell Lowre Few Lane."

He had his nose up in the air, and the rest of us followed him, our hands interlocked. Dylan remained a few paces in front and made a sharp turn then another, and I felt unbelievably lost.

The walls were covered with wanted posters that had pictures of Dylan and Erin. I remembered Brian telling us about them.

"Is Meg still with us?" Jade whispered.

"Ya all are very close," Meg said at our backs.

I followed Dylan through a rectangular doorway and into a spacious open area. There were several colossal-sized werewolf warrior ice sculptures wearing helmets and armor, spread out and standing along the wall. They were over forty feet tall and held axes at their sides.

In the center of the area was a temple with several steps that led to a top. At the peak, a ring radiated blue.

"That must be the portal back to home," Jade said.

"Let's make quick ground, shall we? Imprisoned in a bed of ice is not as much fun as one might think," Meg said.

Dylan and I jogged forward and approached the base of the temple stairs. I tightened my fist over the coin.

A quake erupted, and a major tremor shook the floor under my feet. I pitched forward, and I landed face-first in a pile of snow. Dylan fell on top of me. Jade, Thomas, and Erin were knocked off their feet and piled on top of him. I stared out from the bottom. Meg dropped the gurney and also fell face-first into the snowy ground.

The walls around us gave sharp cracks and snaps. Wide fissures snaked across the surface, and large lumps of ice toppled down. The ice sculpture werewolf warriors' eyes turned a crystal blue and became animated, splitting away from the wall. They surrounded us. We all scrambled back up to our feet and cowered.

One wall buckled, and ice plunged to the ground. A mass force of white wolves sprinted over the rubble and advanced on us, their snouts drawn into snarls. Ice spiders scurried between them and came close.

Spiders and white wolves stepped to the side and made a passageway. Ronan came forward as a werewolf, walking on all fours.

He stepped between the huge feet of an ice sculpture and rose up to his hind legs. Meg stood as well, and Ronan put out his hand. Ice formed over her from neck to feet. He extended out his clawed toes, and my coin rocketed from my hand. He snatched it in the air with a hairy paw.

A sneer spread over Ronan's snout, his sharp, white teeth gleaming. He held out his clawed paw. "Dylan. Erin. Come to me." His voice was grating.

Erin hugged her chest and whimpered. Dylan stared around us, then back to Ronan.

Ronan's grin faltered, and he pointed an index finger. "I'll let them go if you come. And if you don't come willingly..." He flicked one finger, and Thomas's feet were enclosed in ice.

Dylan held his hands up. "O-okay." He turned to me and swallowed. He shifted his gaze up, and there were white swarms in the air. "Aunt Ruth," he breathed.

The horde of white moths fluttered over the snout of one huge ice warrior and then landed to one side of us. Aunt Ruth's body manifested.

A werewolf warrior swung his huge axe down at Aunt Ruth's head, but the moths flittered to and fro, and the blade went through her. The moths reconfigured, and Aunt Ruth was standing a few feet away from the wedged axe head. Ronan growled and held out his hands, sending a bright blue ball bolting toward her. The moths dispersed, swirled in the air, and the lethal sphere went through her, traveling a hundred feet to hit the leg of one mammoth werewolf warrior. It exploded into segments of ice, and I shielded my head as the pieces rained down.

Aunt Ruth's moth-formed body returned, and she held her hands up. "Ronan. You once had a family you loved. These children have families who love them too. Erin has a mother who adores her. And Dylan is my nephew. I love him dearly. But look." She held her hand out to us. "These friends have stuck with Dylan and came for me and Erin. Their hearts are nothing but love. You will rip them away from this family? Your obsessions have made you forget what family truly means."

Ronan's shoulders slouched down. His grin was replaced with an uncertain frown, and in one second, the scary Ronan looked miserable. I couldn't help but feel sorry for him.

Moths fluttered close to Ronan and then whipped over his hand, and the coin he had been holding was gone. He stared down in shock at his empty palm, and the swarm dropped the coin in front of me. Except it was glowing and hovering in the air.

Aunt Ruth turned to us and snapped her fingers. "Use your desires wisely."

Fiery balls zipped out from the floating orb and went into Thomas, Dylan, Jade, and me.

I touched my chest and exchanged looks with everyone. "Let's show Ronan what family is."

I squared my shoulders to Ronan. Memories reeled through my mind of going with my parents on trips, of Georgia cooking her horrible dinners for me. Most importantly, my times with Thomas, Jade, and Dylan were vivid.

I held my hands out. "Realize memories of family."

A purplish orb zipped from my fingers, soared through the air, and hit Ronan straight in the head. Ronan reached up and touched his forehead. His body transformed back to human form, his lips trembled, and a couple of tears spilled from his eyes.

Jade came up and said the same. Then Thomas.

Finally, Dylan stepped up and said, "Realize, see my family in Portland."

All those intimate memories of our families were now in Ronan's mind. He collapsed to his knees between his gray guardian wolves and grabbed his head.

He grimaced in pain and whispered, "Family." He stared up at us. His watery eyes were a bright blue.

I flinched at that look and stepped back. Ronan licked his lips and glanced around in bewilderment.

"What have I done?" He rose to his feet and stared down at his hands. He put his palm up toward Meg. The ice melted away, and she fell to a knee.

Aunt Ruth moaned, sat up, and rubbed her head, her eyes tightly shut. "Blooming headache," she muttered.

Meg grabbed Aunt Ruth and hauled her to her feet.

A nearby werewolf warrior growled in anger and brought his axe back to cut us down. Ronan held up his hands and said, "No. I was wrong. They will go back home."

His two gray wolf guardians stared up at him, their jaws clenched in a snarl. They turned away from him and charged us. Flashes of lightning blew from Ronan's fingertips toward the charging pair. In the next second, the stone wolves were pieces of gray stone lying over the ground.

Ronan shook his head and told us, "You must hurry. I created them and made them feel only darkness. Destruction, I'm afraid it's all they know."

He held his hand out, and a streak of energy flew from his hand, zoomed up the temple steps and hit the blue ring. It turned into a fluorescent turquoise.

I turned to everyone and we all met gazes.

A colossal werewolf warrior advanced toward us and raised its axe. A flash of blue erupted from Ronan's palm, hit the warrior, and there was a sharp crack. I covered my head as chunks showered over me, shards landing close to me. Our path was now clear to the stairs.

Ronan's voice was sharp. "Run!"

I pushed on Erin and Jade to get them moving. Meg hauled Aunt Ruth, and we all reached the top.

Jade pushed on Erin's back. "Go." Erin stepped through the portal.

Meg hollered, "Ya hurry, children, right after me. Not sure how long he can hold them off." She towed Aunt Ruth through. Jade and Thomas looked to me.

I stared down at Ronan. The army Ronan had created were pushing toward him. White wolves, ice spiders, and the colossal werewolf warriors all charged Ronan to get to us.

Ronan defended himself with his own magic, hands raised while flashes erupted from his fingers. There were a series of explosions, and a blanket of whiteness filled my view. The massive army continued its advance, though, and it was clear Ronan would soon be overwhelmed by his own force. Ronan retreated backward step by step to the temple base.

"You know, we each do have one desire left," I said.

Jade smiled and nodded. "You're right, we do. Thomas, let's see how these guys like hockey."

Thomas smiled, stepped forward, and said, "Realize ice skates."

The white wolves, ice spiders, and even large werewolf warrior sculptures all had ice skates formed on their feet in one moment. They looked comically awkward trying to move.

Ronan straightened, brought his hands to his sides, and stared out at the now-clumsy army.

I extended my arms. "Realize boulder-sized hail."

Gigantic pieces of hail rained down from the sky and pummeled into the werewolf warriors, and they were laid to ruins.

"Realize river channel," Dylan said.

Two huge walls of ice pushed out of the ground that enclosed Ronan's army. One wall sprouted up right in front of Ronan. Ronan stepped backward, up a few stairs, and stared in awe at the huge wall in front of him. The channel snaked out to the lake.

"Realize rushing stream," Jade said.

A great deluge of water flooded the channel, swept up the enemy forces, and carried them to the lake. The entire area was left barren.

Ronan wheeled around to us. I held my hand up. Dylan lifted his too. Jade and Thomas did the same.

Ronan's hand came up. A tear crept down a cheek.

Jade turned. "Let's go home, guys."

Thomas stepped through and then Jade. I looked up to Dylan, and he smiled, his dimples apparent. He leaned over and kissed my cheek.

My hand shot to my cheek, and my mouth hung open.

Dylan winked. "You're the best, Colton Ryan." He stepped through the portal.

I rubbed my face and grinned. I took one last gander at Weredom. The silhouette of Ronan walked back toward his castle.

I stepped through the portal and was finally back where this all started. Back in the house at 44 Lowre Few Lane.

Chapter Twenty-Five

I WIPED THE fog from the mirror again and stared at my reflection. A towel was snuggled around my waist, and my wet hair was messed on top. Steam from the hot shower hung heavy in the bathroom.

I combed my hair to one side and styled it for a few seconds. No. I didn't like that. Backward then. That sure didn't work. Parted. Nope. My shoulders slumped. Was I going to figure this out before Dylan and Jade arrived?

There was an abrupt knock on the door, and my father's voice called, "Colton?"

Someone might as well have goosed me hard. I jumped a couple of feet in the air. I closed my eyes for a second and rested my hand on the sink. "Yes, Dad?"

"Open the door."

I cracked the door and the cloudy steam took its opportunity to waft out. My father's face loomed large in the gap, a couple days' beard growth on his face.

"So this boy's aunt is taking you guys to the dance?"

"Yes, Father. And his name is Dylan."

"Right. And Georgia will pick you up. Uh, is Dylan staying over still?"

I nodded.

"Oh," Father said and bumped his head with his palm. "That reminds me. He's here. In fact, they're both downstairs."

"What? They're early!"

Father brought his wrist up, pulled back his sleeve, and revealed his watch. "Okay. Have to go. Remember, Mum will be home Sunday, and we're going to have a special dinner. It'll be better now that she is back home."

I did not know what to say to that. Things seemed fine at the present time.

My father scratched his whiskers, reached through the space in the door to mess up my hair. "I want us to spend more time together. Okay?" He did not wait for an answer but was gone, and I heard him shout, "Have fun at the dance."

Georgia's voice drifted through the door all the way from downstairs. She was fussing over someone, and no doubt a cheek pinching was happening. Dylan's laugh reached my ears.

Panic set in. I combed my hair forward, threaded my fingers through it, and gave it a slightly disheveled look. Perfect. Once in my bedroom, I ripped off my towel and scrambled into my underwear, then put on my trousers, shirt, and dress jacket I had laid out on my bed. My shoes did not cooperate, and I had to sit on the floor and wiggle my feet inside. I hurried down the hallway to the top of the staircase, and Georgia's excited voice came to me. She was complimenting Jade's dress.

I took one step at a time, butterflies in my stomach. Georgia, Dylan, and Jade were standing at the dining room table.

"Mum sewed this up for me last Christmas. Probably be too big soon," Jade told Georgia with a smile.

Georgia put a hand over her mouth and shook her head. "It's amazing."

Dylan's gaze swiveled up and caught mine. A smile crossed Dylan's face, dimples lit up on his cheeks, and he stepped forward. Georgia and Jade looked up at me. Though I'd seen him the day before at school, I was breathless. His hair was brushed back and bangs feathered, and he wore a dark suit with light-blue pinstripes.

"Hey," Dylan said, putting his thumb up. "You, uh, you look really nice, man."

"Me?" That's all I could say. My tongue was there, but it had forgotten how to function.

The television blared in the living room. Georgia had no doubt been watching it. The newscaster reported, "Arklow residents are back to business as usual, one week after a mysterious snow squall. Meteorologists are still investigating..."

Georgia put her hands up over her mouth and spoke between her fingers. "Look at you! Me wee little scab is growing up. You're not so wee anymore, are ya? You're outgrowing that name. Well, your feet stuck in mud? Close that gob of yours before something flies in there and come down here and give us a model walk."

I came down the stairs, ready for the pinching to commence, but Georgia kept both her hands on her chin and grinned. I spun on my toes and held my arms up. *"Ta-da!"*

Jade and Dylan grinned. I noticed Jade's purple-and-black patterned dress for the first time.

"That's quite amazing, Jade."

Georgia patted Jade's shoulder. "She's most beautiful, isn't she?"

There was a knock on the door. "Oh, that's my aunt, I bet. She went to run an errand while you were getting ready." Dylan opened the door, and Aunt Ruth stood on the front porch. She was dressed in jeans and a wool shirt, staring over Dylan's head with a smirk across her face at seeing all of us.

"Well, invite the poor woman in, and I'll make us some tea," Georgia called out.

Aunt Ruth held her hands up. "Oh, that's kind. I promised them ice cream before the dance, though. I think we're running out of time."

Georgia peered at the clock in the corner of the room and flapped her hand at me. "Oh, my. It is late. You better get going."

Aunt Ruth held the door open for us. "How's that headache you had last week?" she asked Georgia.

Georgia touched her forehead and shook her head. "Oh my. That was quite a nasty bugger. I think it was something I ate. My mind was foggy for a bit, but thanks to that tea you gave me, it straightened right up."

Aunt Ruth smiled, and her eyes twinkled. "I'm so glad to hear that. Well, we should go out for tea sometime on the square. I know a good place." She waved and made more pleasantries.

I stepped over to Dylan and Jade who waited by the car. I couldn't help but grin from ear to ear.

Jade laughed. "What are you so happy about?"

Dylan smirked. I cocked my head to the side and frowned at her.

She laughed and looked to both of us. "I think you both will be the cutest couple."

I sighed. "Too bad we can't dance together."

Dylan swatted my arm. "*I know*. We can cut the lights and do a quick dance in the dark."

Jade nodded. "Brilliant. Then you'd probably cut the music out too."

"Oh," Dylan said, shrugging. "Oopsies. Forgot about that."

Aunt Ruth came up, scanned us, and turned to Jade. "You look stunning, dear." Then to Dylan and me. "Very good-looking gentlemen." She held her hand out toward the car doors. "Shall we? Better hit the road."

Two ice cream scoops later and an accidental spill on Jade's dress, followed by vigorous scrubbing, Aunt Ruth dropped us off in front of the gym.

We got out of the car, and Dylan kissed her cheek and told her with a smile, "Later, gator."

Aunt Ruth regarded him warmly from the driver seat and then considered all of us. She looked to be contemplating something.

"I never said after last week, but thank you for everything, kids. You were very brave. I have no words."

Dylan and Jade shifted on their feet. I stepped up. "Well, thank you for giving Georgia that lemon tea. You helped her forget we were not home when she woke up on the couch."

A smirk twitched at the end of her mouth. "The least I could do."

She turned to Dylan and became stern. "Heard tonight there's a full moon. Best if you keep everything under control." Her eyes softened. "But if you do let loose, stay close to Jade and Colton so they think you're their pet." She smiled and drove away.

We stood there for a moment, held in comfortable silence, as her car drove down the street and turned a corner. Some boys were walking up, and I recognized John and a couple of rugby players. John's eyes lit up at seeing Dylan, and he trotted to us. I received a cursory and suspicious glimpse.

"Dylan, mate. Come hang out with us inside."

My stomach tightened, and my body tensed. Dylan bumped fists with John, a new fad that had spread through the school.

"Wha's up, man," Dylan said and looked to me. "Be in in a second."

I nodded, and Jade and I walked up to the front door. Something swelled inside me and anger frothed up. I glanced over my shoulder. Dylan was talking to the boys, and they laughed.

"What's wrong, Colton?" Jade asked.

I turned to her and shook my head, not wanting to discuss the jealous anger rising. I opened the door, let Jade inside, and stepped into the foyer while wringing my hands. He was going to hang out with them, and I'd be alone.

She leaned up to my ear and whispered, "After everything, you have doubt he'd hang out with you?"

I looked away. Tears welled up in my eyes. I was a nerd at school, someone good at maths, but that was it.

Or was it?

The memories of the previous week reeled through my mind. Dylan chasing the wolf pack away and saving Jade, Erin, and me. Going to the hospital. Sliding down an icy hill to 44 Lowre Few and going inside a decrepit house and then a portal. Laughing inside an igloo with a snow squall outside. Racing across an iced-over lake on a sleigh...

Something unexpected happened. My tense emotions deflated. Jade was right. Dylan and I were bonded in a way that was extraordinary and unlike any other friends. Who else got into a magical realm with their friends to defeat a sorcerer? I'm pretty sure this was a first. I really had nothing to worry about.

I turned to Jade and smiled. "You're right."

She put her arm around my back and gave me a squeeze. "About time you recognize that."

I took a moment to admire the orange and black balloons in the gym, a few elaborate Hallow's Eve decorations. "You and Erin did this?"

Jade laughed. "And a few others. And oh, Thomas too. He's quite creative."

"Where is Thomas?"

Jade pointed, and I observed a mess of red hair towering over other students and coming toward me. Erin was with him, her hand resting at the crook of his elbow.

Thomas punched my shoulder. "When you scallywags arrive?"

I bopped his arm. "Just got here, ya scallywag." I looked to Erin.

A smile beamed on her face, the gap in her teeth conspicuous as always. "Hey, Colton." She looked over my shoulder, surveyed the area, and met my eyes. "Where's Dylan? Thought you guys were coming together?"

Thomas pointed over my shoulder. "There's the rascal."

I turned as Dylan sauntered over, an easy smile on his face. My heart lifted seeing him, and I stared at his face as he bumped fists with Thomas and kissed Erin's cheek.

"Wha's up, guys?"

Thomas pointed upward. "From the looks of it, balloons." He honked out laughter.

Headmaster Collins announced a welcome message from the stage, and students in the gym looked in his direction. The lights dimmed, and Dylan turned his attention to the headmaster. I marveled at Dylan and considered every minute detail from the tip of his nose to the thickness of his brow. He turned to me, met my eyes, and smiled. His fingers dusted mine, and he nestled closer.

"What did you tell the lads?" I whispered.

He offered me a lopsided grin. "Made a disclosure."

"Crikey! You said you were gay?"

Dylan rolled his eyes. "No, I told them I was a werewolf." He swatted my chest. "Of course, I told them I was gay."

My face felt hot. "That was rash. H-how did they take it?"

He shrugged. "I think they were surprised. But we'll see how it goes."

Loud music started up. It was hip-hop, and a few students started dancing. Several stepped toward the sides. Jade, Thomas, Erin, Dylan, and I made our way to the center, and I pumped my fists and wiggled my body. Dylan, of course, was a natural at dancing, and he gyrated in fluid motion and pivoted around in circles.

A plump girl caught my attention. She came onto the dance floor wearing a neon-green outfit, her moves fluid and fast. The students made a circle around her and clapped their hands, and we watched her.

Thomas looked over to me and pushed my arm and yelled something.

"What?" I shouted back.

He pointed to the girl who was now spinning on the top of her head, met with hearty applause. "*IT'S MEG!*"

I snapped my focus back to the dancer. It was indeed Meg. I had not seen her since we'd walked back into 44 Lowre Few Lane. Aunt Ruth had made a new portal inside the house and had gone back home, or so I'd thought.

I clapped my hands harder and guffawed. The song ended, and the students roared with raucous laughter and ovations; multiple hands reached out and patted her on the back.

Meg came up to me. Jade, Dylan, and Thomas stood at my side as I yelled, "What are you doing here?"

Meg grinned, put her hand up to her mouth, and shouted back. "Came on vacation." She pointed down at her clothes. "Like it? Aunt Ruth got it for me."

I exchanged looks with Jade, Thomas, and Dylan. Not the sort of attire I ever wore, but maybe it fit for her.

Thomas put his hand up to his mouth. "Off the hook."

I laughed out loud, and Meg smiled and performed a new twist on the floor. Sweat trickled down my spine, and the music roared on. Dylan spun with his hands pumping up in the air in rhythm with the music, and girls and boys clapped and laughed. Ms. Griffin was standing on one side of the room, watching us dance, and she wiggled her hips in time with the music.

A slow dance came on and several students who had been gyrating froze in place, looked around in confusion, and scampered off the dance floor. Meg kissed my cheek and then Dylan's, Jade's, and Thomas's.

Several boys asked Meg, and she put a hand over her eyes, stuck a finger out and spun, stopping on a lanky, thin boy. Thomas and Erin joined hands, pressed up against one another. Erin lay her head on his chest, and they swayed to the music. A boy asked Jade for a dance, and she accepted.

I stepped off with Dylan. It was Arklow, Ireland, and two boys dancing might cause a bit of an uproar. We stepped into the shadows, and Dylan took my hand. My breath caught.

Dylan turned to me and didn't look away. I wanted to kiss him. We were in a crowd, though, and that was impossible.

He brought his hand up and said, "Might be a good time for a fire drill."

"What?" I stared down at his palm. A gold coin lay there.

A smirk formed on my face. "Meg just gave it to me and said it was enchanted and worked the same as it did in her world. Just need to say the word."

My smirk transformed into a grin.

"Realize our dance."

About the Author

Bryce was raised by his mother and father in the countryside near Wichita, Kansas and learned to become an avid reader from his mother and maternal grandfather who carries the last name of Bentley. Stephen King novels still stack his two shelves in his old bedroom at home. After graduating from his high school with a class size of 69, he completed college where he had never came out gay, then took a winding journey over his entire 20s. This took him to Indiana, then to the San Francisco Bay Area where he still did not come out but obtained a master's degree. He traveled to Bangkok, Thailand during his late 20s to teach English for a year and he met his first boyfriend. Five years later, he completed his doctorate degree in psychology, which was inspired by a youth and young adulthood of feeling internally bewildered. Bryce started dabbling in writing in 2011 or in his mid-thirties. He self-published several works under his name over the last few years, but it was in 2016 he felt like he was finally getting the hang of this writing thing. The Werewolf on Lowre Few Lane is his first work under his pen name of Bryce Bentley-Tales. His next YA novel with a working title of Orion: The PreRobo Era Boy, is a work he is finishing up currently. Bryce currently lives in Dallas, Texas.

Website: www.brycebentleytales.com

Twitter: @BryceTales

Facebook: www.facebook.com/YALGBTauthor

Email: brycebentleytales@yahoo.com

Also Available from NineStar Press

Connect with NineStar Press

Website: NineStarPress.com

Facebook: NineStarPress

Facebook Reader Group: NineStarNiche

Twitter: @ninestarpress

Tumblr: NineStarPress

www.ingramcontent.com/pod-product-compliance
Lightning Source LLC
Chambersburg PA
CBHW060556190726
48283CB00003B/1039